MW01470467

Summertime Forgiveness

An Oak Harbor Series

Kimberly Thomas

Prologue

One year ago

"Guys, breakfast is ready!" Jo called out to her family as she pulled back to admire the spread she'd prepared for them. On the table lay eggs, bacon, English sausages, croissant, French toast, hash browns, muffins, a dish with freshly made strawberry jam, and a tray of fruits. The dark liquid in the coffee maker slowly trickled into the receptacle, waiting to catch it on the kitchen counter.

She felt a pair of hands pull her into a firm chest before a soft kiss was placed against her temple, making her shiver with pleasure.

"Good morning, beautiful," her husband's raspy voice whispered against her ear.

Jo placed her palm against his cheek tenderly.

"Hi, honey," she replied softly. "How was your sleep?"

Jo felt herself being turned around until she was facing him. Charles tilted her face upward so that she was looking into his chocolate brown eyes.

"I slept extremely well," he informed her. "Why didn't you wake me? I could have helped you with all of this." His gaze swept past her to the display on the table.

"You looked so peaceful. It felt like a sin to disturb you considering how hard you've been working these few months," she told him. She brought her hands up to wrap them around his neck as she slightly pulled him down to her—her intention clear.

"Eww! Get a room."

Jo pulled away from her husband and moved her head to the side to look behind him. Charles turned his torso a little to look also.

Their seventeen-year-old son stood by the stairs, looking at them with mock disgust.

"Close your eyes if it's too much for you," his father retorted before turning back to Jo and firmly enclosing her in his arms once more before his lips were on hers, kissing her soundly.

Jo laughed against his lips at the gagging sounds Nicholas made behind them.

"Don't worry, Son. When you find the one person you can't live without, you won't be able to keep your lips or hands to yourself," Charles threw over his shoulder as he smiled down at his wife.

"That won't be anytime soon, though," their son returned.

"Definitely not," Jo agreed readily. "You've got your whole life ahead of you to get it right," she finished.

Just then, their daughter Tracy came bounding down the stairs. She stopped by her brother and looked from him to her parents in confusion.

"What'd I miss?" she asked, walking over to her parents. Nicholas did the same.

"Nothing much, sweetie. Only your brother interrupting me giving your mother the perfect good-morning kiss," Charles explained.

"Sounds boring," Tracy replied, moving toward the table that had her full attention.

"Wow, Mom. You outdid yourself today. What's the occasion?" she asked, popping a piece of fruit in her mouth.

Jo finally separated from her husband and turned to her daughter.

"No occasion, sweetie. I'm off from the restaurant for the next two days, and I just wanted to do something special for all of you," she informed her.

"Oh, that's great. Maybe you could help me with a few recipes that I could make for Josh, you know, for when we move in together," Tracy suggested as she took a seat.

"Did you say recipe? Don't you mean poison?"

"Shut up, Nick!" Tracy seethed, not appreciative of her brother's comments.

"Nicholas, be nice to your sister," Jo implored her son as she too went to take a seat at the table.

"I can't help it, Mom. She makes it too easy," Nicholas snickered.

"God, you're such a child," Tracy said with a roll of her eyes.

Jo smiled at her children, enjoying their time together that would soon come to an end with her daughter moving in with her boyfriend. She knew the two would miss each other even if their constant bickering suggested otherwise. They always had each other's back.

"All right, guys, be nice. Your mother went through a lot of trouble to make breakfast for you, so please don't argue at the table," their father stepped in.

The siblings stopped their back and forth but kept giving each other death glares.

"You're not staying to have breakfast with us?" Jo asked as he added Saran Wrap to the plate in his hand, packed with food.

"I can't. I need to get to the office. I have to get through some important paperwork that I've neglected," he explained. "But I'll be home early."

"Okay, honey." Jo rose from her seat and went over to grab the travel cup from the cupboard before pouring the hot dark liquid into it. She then handed it to her husband.

Charles took the cup before pecking her lips. "Thank you."

Jo smiled lovingly at him. "You look really good, by the way, scrumptious even," she complimented, running her hands down the lapels of his jacket.

"Oh yeah, you think so?" Charles asked, batting his eyelashes daintily.

This elicited a laugh from her as she lightly tapped his chest.

"I'll see you later," she spoke, reaching up to kiss him again.

"Hey, you two. Break it up," Nicholas interrupted their moment. "Dad, can I get a ride with you later, please? I'm going by the dentist to get my wisdom tooth pulled this afternoon, so I'll be in your neck of the woods."

"Sure thing, Son," Charles replied, reaching down to take his briefcase from the floor where he had placed it. "Just come by the office when you're done."

Jo stood by the front door, watching her husband pull out of the garage and onto the street. Charles tooted his horn as he waved goodbye. She waved at the man who had been the love of her life and her best friend for the past twenty years as a warm smile graced her lips. She pulled her cardigan around her as she watched the car drive down the street until it disappeared.

When she stepped back inside, she could hear the raised voices of her children as they traded insults. Jo shook her head as she made her way toward the kitchen/dining room.

"Shut up, dork!"

"All right, guys. That's enough fighting for the day. You two need to learn to get along more. Soon you won't be under the same roof, and I know you'll miss each other despite your behavior toward each other," Jo chided her children as she took a seat at the table.

Both looked at their mother with remorse.

"Sorry, Mom. It's just Nick rubs me the wrong way, and his jokes aren't even that funny," Tracy rationalized. "But I'll be the bigger person. I'm sorry, Nicholas, for calling you a couch potato with no social life." Tracy smirked at her brother.

Nicholas opened his mouth to respond, but Jo quickly held up her hand, halting whatever insult she knew he was about to throw back at his sister under the guise of an apology. "Let's just eat first, and then you can go back to what you were doing before." Her children nodded in agreement.

After grace, everyone dug into the food before them, taking as much as they could consume.

"Mom, you really went all out with this. It makes me excited to see what you'll make later," Tracy complimented.

"It won't be such a surprise," Jo returned.

Tracy looked across the table at her mother, her brown eyes so reflective of her mother's, filled with question.

"You're going to help me prepare it," Jo explained. "Look at this as the beginning of your practice for when you move into your apartment with Josh."

Tracy never had the patience to sit and help with the cooking and always had an excuse as to why she couldn't help in the kitchen. Jo hadn't forced her, knowing that when the time came, she would probably seek her out for assistance. It appeared that time had come. She would be living with her boyfriend Josh in an apartment closer to the University of Washington Tacoma, where she would be attending come this fall. Even though they lived in Tacoma, the university was located on Commerce Street, and the family house was further north-eastern in the Proctor District. Tracy had presented her argument that she was now an adult and should be able to make her own decisions concerning how the rest of her life would go. Charles had given his blessing on her decision, and Jo had begrudgingly given hers too.

"By the way, how is the move coming along? Do you need any help?"

"No thanks, Mom. Josh came by yesterday to help me get the last of my things into boxes. He carried a few of them in his jeep, but the movers are coming tomorrow to move the rest," Tracy informed her mother.

Jo gave her daughter a small smile. "Sounds like you're all set."

"I'll visit every chance I get to. I promise," Tracy appeased her mother, having picked up on the shift in her mood.

Jo reached across the table and gave her daughter's hand a gentle squeeze.

"Sure, you will, Sis. It's not like you'll be able to live on ramen forever."

Tracy turned to glare at her brother.

"Nicholas." Jo sighed tiredly.

Hearing this, Nicholas threw up his hands. "All right, I'm done. I promise," he replied in surrender. "Truth be told. I'm really going to miss you, Sis," he spoke sincerely before ducking his head, avoiding eye contact.

At this, Tracy moved her chair closer before pulling him to her side with her arm over his shoulders. "I'll miss you, too, twerp. You're the best annoying little brother a girl could ever have."

"Hey, you're not that much older than me," Nicholas tried to correct his sister, wriggling out of her arm.

"Doesn't matter. I'm still older than you," Tracy rebutted.

And just like that, the tender moment they had just shared disappeared with their arguing.

Jo smiled fondly at her two children. She loved them more than the world. She loved her husband. She loved her life.

* * *

"Didn't Dad say he would be home early?" Tracy asked her mother as she helped her set the table for their dinner. "I thought that meant before dinner time."

"He should be home soon," Jo confirmed. The time on the wall clock read 6:15. She was used to Charles coming home at late hours of the night, but he had promised he would be home early, and the fact that he was Nicholas's ride home, she determined he should have been home by now.

Just then, her phone pinged. Snatching it from the table, she read the message displayed on the screen.

"Well, I guess it's just the two of us this evening, sweetie," she sighed.

Tracy looked back at her mother expectantly.

"Charles got delayed. He said his boss sprang a meeting on him last minute, so we should go ahead and eat. He and Nick will grab something to hold them over before they get home."

"Oh," Tracy replied, disappointed.

Jo knew how she probably felt. She had hoped they could dine together as a family— they hadn't had one of those in months now. With Charles always working late and Jo's schedule being rotational, it had been difficult for them to sit with their children to just eat and talk about their day.

The two women sat in silence eating, each lost in their own thoughts.

"Why don't we watch a movie," Tracy suggested after they washed the dishes.

"Sure, what do you have in mind?" Jo asked, not ready to call it a night and happy that her daughter suggested an activity that could have them spending more time together.

Tracy tapped her chin in thought. "How about *A nightmare on Elm Street*?"

"No way. You know I don't have the stomach for anything too gory, sweetheart," Jo declined.

"Okay, then take it away. What do you suggest?"

The two finally settled on the plush wraparound couch in the family room as the movie *Sweet Home Alabama* played on the television. Two hours later, the doorbell rang. Tracy rose to go get it, but Jo stopped her.

"I'll go."

As Jo went to answer the door, she wondered who it was at this hour of the night. Opening the door, she was surprised to see two police officers standing before her there, the blue and red lights flashing in the background. She felt her heart clench as her fingers tightened around the door.

"Good evening, Officers. How may I help you?"

"Good evening, ma'am. Are you Mrs. Jo Hamilton-Boyer?" one of the officers asked grimly.

"Ye-yes, I am," she confirmed.

The two officers paused and looked between each other before looking back at her, their eyes filled with sympathy.

It felt like an eternity before either one of them spoke, and Jo felt the air being sliced off from her lungs before they even uttered the words that would haunt her for the rest of her life. July 17 would be a date she never forgot.

"I'm sorry to inform you, ma'am, but your husband was in an accident this evening. He lost control of his car and hit a tree. He and a young male that was in the passenger seat, we believe to be your son, died on impact."

There was a guttural cry of pain behind her, but she couldn't turn to go and comfort her daughter. She remained transfixed, unable to process what had just been said. Shortly after, there was a ringing in her ears before everything went blank, and she fainted.

Chapter One

Present Day

Jo walked up the stairs toward the set of bedrooms on the upper floor of her home. She popped her head into the first room, which had been her daughter's before she'd finally moved out just over six months ago. Satisfied that nothing was left out, she bypassed the other bedroom across from it and instead went to the guest room beside it to ensure that, like her daughter's room, nothing had been left out.

She made her way to the master bedroom at the end of the hall. She paused with her hand on the doorknob for a good minute before turning it and entering the space. The room was empty, stripped of all the things that had made it a safe haven up until one year ago. She quickly walked toward the en-suite bathroom to make sure she had removed all her toiletries and products from off the counters and her pills from the medicine cabinet.

Sucking in a deep breath, then releasing it, she made a hasty retreat from the room and headed for the stairs at the opposite end. As if an invisible force had stopped her descent, she turned back to the only room she had not entered, her son's bedroom. Josephine held the doorknob, but she did not turn it. Her knuckles turned white from how tightly she held on. Her head dropped until her forehead rested against the hard wood of the door. Finally getting the courage, she opened the door and quickly scanned the room without entering before pulling it shut. Her heart beat erratically against her ribcage. She made her way down the stairs and went into the kitchen to grab her sports bottle, the only one out, and filled it with water. After gulping down most of the liquid, she made her way to the family room to finish.

After what seemed like forever, Jo sighed heavily as she stepped back from the last box she had just packed and taped. The movers would be coming soon to put the things she wouldn't be taking with her to storage.

She ran her fingers over the now bare walls of the family room. These walls once held frames that displayed the family portraits and created the perfect backdrop behind the gray five-piece sectional sofa that took up a considerable amount of space. The large flat-screen television hung on the opposite wall above the mahogany entertainment unit with the protruding brick-themed fireplace on the wall adjacent. This room held so many memories. Her mind shifted to a happy one, and a small smile graced her lips.

The whole family had sat on the couch, so close that they were all touching in some way, their eyes glued to the television. A large bowl of popcorn and glasses of juice lay on the coffee table before them. Charles had his hand over Jo's shoulder, his fingers gently caressing her upper arm. Tracy had her head in her mother's lap while Nicholas's head rested on his sister's side. It was such a rarity to see them so close without being at each other's throats. Jo ran her hand through Nicholas's short, curly brunette hair. Content was the best word she could find to express how she felt at that moment.

Just like that, her nostalgia became too much to bear, and she couldn't stay in the room anymore. It was now a room like the many others that reminded her of the pain— the loss she had to endure. The loss she'd been holding on to.

As she walked through the other rooms of the house, she'd called home for more than eighteen years. She couldn't help the tears that welled up in her eyes as her memories of what was and would no longer be, took preeminence over everything else. God, how she missed them. She still hadn't gotten over the grief of losing her husband and her son just a year ago. Every time her mind went back to the day she received the news, it always left her reeling as if she was there again. It had gotten even worse after the one-year anniversary just last month.

This had been the greatest factor that led to her making the decision to sell the house and the fact that she needed to be there for her sick mother now that her father was no longer alive to do it.

* * *

"Mom?"

Tracy's voice echoed off the now empty walls of the house and pulled Jo out of her melancholy thoughts.

"In here, sweetie," she called up from the basement.

Shortly after, she heard her daughter's footsteps falling against the wooden stairs.

"What are you doing down here?" Tracy asked curiously as soon as she moved off the last step.

Jo tried to plaster on a smile, not wanting to worry her daughter, whose concerned gaze was fixed on her.

"I was just trying to see if I could get some of these things upstairs," she explained, gesturing to the boxes packed with her husband's gym equipment.

Tracy's toffee brown eyes widened in alarm at her mother. "Mom, these are way too heavy for you to handle alone. Why didn't you wait until I got here, or better yet, leave it for the movers to get? It's their job, after all."

Jo sighed. "I just— I needed to do something to keep me occupied and..."

Tracy nodded in understanding before reaching over to hug her mother, her head of brunette locks resting against her chest. Jo hugged her daughter tightly against her. At that moment, it felt as if Tracy was the only thing keeping her tethered to this life, and if she let her go, she would crumble into an abyss of perpetual sorrow.

When it felt safe enough, Jo separated from her daughter and gave her a grateful smile, one that Tracy returned, although she could see it in her eyes that her thoughts too had traveled to the tragedy that had taken her father and her brother in an instant.

"I brought food. I hope you're hungry," Tracy spoke, turning her head to hide what her mother had already seen.

"Thank you, honey. I actually do have a bit of an appetite," Jo replied.

The two women left the basement and found themselves in the empty living room where Tracy had left the takeout bag on one of the boxes.

"So, what'd you get?" Jo asked.

"Your favorite," Tracy replied as she grabbed the bag.

"Smoked leg of a lamb?"

"Try again. It's something both of us love," Tracy encouraged her mother.

"Sushi," Jo said instantly.

Tracy bobbed her head excitedly before removing the contents of the bag.

"Where can we eat?" she asked, looking around the furniture-less room.

"Right here." Jo pointed to the floor before lowering herself onto it.

After handing the food to her mother, Tracy followed suit and sat across from her.

Jo began to salivate as soon as she opened the covered container to see the array of choices her daughter had gotten her. There were maki, temaki, uramaki, rigiri and sashimi. The scent of the fresh fish intermingled with the spices used to make the rolls assayed her senses.

"Mm, these smells wonderful," she gushed, casting her gaze over to her daughter. "Thanks, sweetie."

Tracy gave her a warm smile before digging into her own plate.

Jo moaned in pleasure the second she placed the roll into her mouth. Her taste buds were bursting with a plethora of flavors, from the mild flavor of the salmon topping to the delicate sweet and sour taste of the peach slices embedded in the seaweed-wrapped rice cake and the slightly tangy, slightly salty soy sauce dip.

"Mandolin?" she asked, referring to the sushi and steak house they used to frequent often.

"You know it couldn't have been from anywhere else, Mom," Tracy confirmed with a grin.

The two settled in comfortable silence as they continued to enjoy their meal.

"So, are you ready for college?" Jo finally broke the silence to ask her daughter. Tracy had deferred her acceptance to study journalism at the University of Washington Tacoma for a year after the accident but would be attending in the fall.

Tracy stopped eating to answer her mother. "I am," she said as her mouth widened into a smile, then it dropped as a troubled look flitted across her face. "But I'm also nervous." Tracy looked down at her plate and sighed.

Jo waited for her to continue.

"I know it's only been a year, yet it feels like it's been longer, and I'm having these thoughts that I won't be able to keep up. Josh says it's just precollege jitters and that it'll pass as soon as I officially start," Tracy confessed.

Jo gave her daughter a look of understanding. "Josh may just be right, and I want to add that you are already a very smart and talented young woman, and I am confident that you will do well."

Tracy gave her mother a grateful smile. "Thanks, Mom. I really needed to hear that."

Jo leaned over to take her daughter's hand in hers and gave it an encouraging squeeze that Tracy returned.

"How is my handsome son-in-law, by the way?" she asked.

At this, the light in Tracy's eyes returned. "Josh is great. He's been so wonderful, and sometimes I don't know what I did to deserve him."

Jo understood that giddy feeling her daughter was experiencing toward her fiancé. It was the same way she had felt about Tracy's father— unable to prevent a smile from forming on her lips or the butterflies from making an appearance whenever she thought or spoke about him. Her daughter was in love, and she was happy for her. She prayed Josh would never do anything to cause her daughter to lose the stars that she carried in her eyes for him. Her smile wavered, and her heart clenched as her thoughts ventured away from the present.

"His granddad is thinking of retiring and leaving the dealership to him as early as next year."

Her daughter's excitement broke through her reverie. Jo willed her smile to return. "That is wonderful news, sweetie. I'm happy for him, for both of you," she congratulated.

Tracy beamed at her mother. "So, have you told Grandma

and Aunt Cora and Andrea that you're moving back to Oak Harbor?" she asked after a beat.

"No, not yet." Jo confessed. "I want it to be a surprise." She had decided to return to her childhood home to help her sisters take care of the family business and their sick mother, but even up to last week, she wondered if the decision was a wise one considering the history with her family. It was true that after the funeral, they had made up after more than twenty years apart, but it still felt as if they were all strangers, and she wasn't sure how their dynamics would go once she returned. Still, it was a better choice than remaining in a city that reminded her so much with every turn she made of all that she'd lost last year. So, after selling the house, she quit her job and was now preparing herself to drive home.

After finishing their meals, Tracy helped her mother to get the last of her luggage into the tailgate of her matte green RAV4.

"I love you, Mom. Please drive safe." Tracy hugged her mother tightly.

Jo brought her hand up to rub it against her daughter's long hair. "I love you, too, sweetie. I'll call you when I get there."

When the two separated, Jo entered her car and started the engine. She looked over and gave her daughter one last warm smile that Tracy returned.

"I'll visit for Grandma's birthday and maybe stay for a week," Tracy informed her mother before stepping away from the car.

"Okay, sweetie. See you in a few weeks." Jo slowly backed out of the driveway before waving goodbye to her daughter and taking off for the highway.

Chapter Two

The minute Jo's car passed the sign, "Welcome to Whidbey Island," she felt her heart clench with anticipation. She hadn't been driving through the town for more than a few minutes, and already she felt the telltale signs of her flight mode kicking in. Her father's funeral was three months ago, but with the way she was feeling, it might as well have been just yesterday. It was that same feeling that had clamored at her heart, telling her that she needed to get away from here.

She hadn't been in contact with her father for more than twenty years up to his death. Still, the feeling of loss had been magnified by the loss of Charles and Nicholas. Unlike her disposition at their funeral, where she'd been numb for the whole service, courtesy of medication prescribed by her MD, the moment she had entered the church for his funeral, she'd felt herself shattering to pieces, and at the end, when she went to say her final goodbye, she almost crumpled and fell to the floor if Cora hadn't held on to her.

"All right, Jo, get it together. Everything will be fine. You can do this," she pep-talked herself as her brown eyes stared back at her from the rearview mirror.

Ten minutes later, Jo turned onto the long winding path that led to the family property. The path was hedged in by tall trees on either side, their long, thin branches stretching across each other into a canopy of their dense foliage, forming a tunnel.

The tunnel opened up to the rest of the pathway being hedged in by fire and ice daylilies, anemone, and bomb lilies, further supported by low-cut boxwood. Beyond this was lush greenery for as far as the eyes could see. The uniformity of the terrain only broken by a tree or a shrub here and there and the thick, forested area bordering the property and blocking out most of the view of the harbor.

Shortly after, she was driving past the three-story colonial home that had been transformed into an inn. It had already been passed down five generations in her family, her and her sisters making it six since their father had left it to them. The architecture was one to be marveled at, and with the few additions that she could see were made to it, she was certain it could rival any of the top inns across the country.

She passed the barn house that had been transformed into a restaurant. Even with its rustic-looking exterior, it had an inviting aura about it that called out to the sous chef in her. She would be visiting this spot regularly, she was sure.

When she pulled up to the house five minutes later, the sun was poised to disappear behind the horizon painting the sky orange along with everything else in its path.

Jo stepped out of her car and looked up at the two-story building she grew up in. Not much had changed in the past twenty years. Except for the change of color, everything looked the same. She made her way up the steps that led to the porch, drawing her luggage along. She went to ring the doorbell when the sound of laughter that seemed to be coming from the back of the house caught her attention.

Leaving her belongings by the door, she walked around the wraparound porch until she came upon her mother, her sisters, and her niece Aurora. Cora and her mother were on the porch swing that moved gently back and forth while Andrea and Aurora sat in bamboo chairs looking out at the harbor. The sun that was now halfway down lightly tinted the water, which was darkened by the absence of the full spectrum of light. Each woman had a glass of wine in their hands.

"I hope you left some wine for me," she spoke, breaking her family out of their conversation.

"Jo," Andrea said excitedly, getting out of her chair to hug her sister.

Jo held her sister tightly. "Hi, Drea."

Shortly after Andrea released her, she felt another pair of hands pull her into another embrace. This time it was Cora. "I'm happy you're here, sweetie," she murmured against her ear, rubbing her back before releasing. The look of joy reflected in her sister's eyes told her that her words were sincere.

The next person that hugged her was her niece. "It's good to see you, Aunt Jo," she expressed when they separated.

"It's good to see you too, Rory," she returned, reaching out to sift a strand of the girl's ginger-colored hair through her index and middle finger. "How is that wonderful fiancé of yours?" she asked.

At this, an even brighter smile graced the young woman's face as her emerald eyes glinted. It reminded Jo so much of Tracy's own expressions when talking about Josh.

"James's great. He's still in San Francisco working on a big case," Rory explained.

"That's wonderful," she replied, delighted.

"Hi, Mom," she greeted Becky, who was a few feet away from her but looked at her with cautious eyes. "How are you?"

"I'm okay, sweetie." Becky gave her daughter a small smile as she walked toward her. "Better, now that you're all here," she revealed before taking her youngest daughter into her arms and hugging her gently.

Jo hugged her mother carefully as if she were a delicate flower that would crumble if she held her any other way. "I'm glad you're doing okay," she murmured against her mother's hair before pulling away.

"Why didn't you tell us you were coming? We could have prepared your old room and probably ordered something from the restaurant," Cora asked as she leaned against the porch railing.

"That's fine. I'm still full from the last meal I ate," she assured her sister. "Besides, I wanted it to be a surprise," she finished.

"Well, it worked," Andrea chimed in. "A pleasant surprise, though," she finished, bringing the glass to her lips and taking a sip of the dark liquid within.

"I think I need one of those," Jo said, pointing to the glass in her sister's hand.

"Of course," Andrea replied. "Let me just go get a glass so you can enjoy this goodness."

"No, stay." Jo stopped her movements. "I'll go get it. I need to bring in my luggage from off the front porch."

"Are you sure you don't need any help?" Cora offered.

"No, it's fine. It's not that heavy," she assured her.

With that, Jo pushed the side door open and entered the dining room. She walked toward the foyer separated by the columns and the arched open doorway. She passed the stairs and came upon the center table with the ceramic vase in the foyer. She remembered Andrea had broken it, but all three sisters had glued it back together. Although they hadn't done that great of a job, the fact that it was still the focal point of the table warmed her heart in that it was kept there after all these years. It was as if the history of her childhood years had been preserved with how many things remained the same, unchanged— like her bedroom, the old swing out by the oak tree a few feet away from the house, and the markings on the height chart displaying the last height recorded for each sister by the wall across from the stairs. An appreciative grin graced her lips as the nostalgia overwhelmed her.

Jo left her luggage at the foot of the stairs before heading to the kitchen to grab a glass. When she made it back outside, everyone was seated in their original positions once more. Jo reached for one of the empty bamboo chairs and placed it beside Andrea's.

Andrea lifted the bottle of merlot and poured it into Jo's waiting glass until it was half full. She smiled with gratitude at her sister before raising the glass to her lips.

"So, what have I missed?" she asked after taking a few sips of the alcoholic beverage.

"Well, Jamie is finally finished with the gazebo behind the inn, and it is beautiful. The dock is also finished, and you won't believe this, but he restored Dad's old boat. It looks so brand new and sleek," Cora gushed as she filled her sister in about the changes that had taken place since her return.

"Sounds like someone is a huge fan of the man's work," Jo mused as she noted how excited Cora sounded talking about Jamie.

"He's a great contractor and a good man," Cora continued to say.

"And boyfriend, don't forget to add that," Andrea added with a smirk.

"Drea," Cora jumped in with a look of warning.

"What, are you two an item now?" Jo said in surprise.

"We're dating," Cora confirmed. "But we decided to take it slow," she hurried to add.

"That sounds wonderful, Cora. I'm happy that you're

putting yourself out there again. You deserve to be happy," Jo assured her sister.

"Thanks, Jo." Cora looked down at her sister with a smile. Jo returned her smile.

A peaceful quietness fell over the women as they looked out into the dark of the night, sipping their refill of wine. Their mother had only had a few sips on account of the medications she was on, but the others indulged heavily in the fruity wine. Now and again, the conversation would pick up before dying down again. Such was the cadence of the evening.

Becky, Aurora, and Andrea decided to call it a night, but Jo and Cora remained out on the porch, not ready to head inside.

"I sold my house," Jo confessed, turning her head to look at her sister, gauging her reaction.

Cora stared bug-eyed at her sister. "That was... unexpected," she replied cautiously. "What made you sell?"

Jo turned away from her sister's searching eyes. "I needed to. With Charles and Nicholas gone and Tracy starting school and her new life... it just didn't make sense living there all by myself," she explained. "Not with all the memories..." she softly added before bringing the wineglass to her lips and finishing the drink in one gulp.

She heard the chair beside her slightly creak before her sister's warm fingers intertwined with hers and squeezed in reassurance.

"I'm sorry you had to go through it all by yourself, Jo. I wish I had done more, reached out more, and come around more. I want to be here for you now, any way you need, just tell me, and I will," Cora expressed, her tone pleading as the guilt from not being there during those hard months for her sister plagued her.

"Thanks, Cora. It means a lot to have you in my life again. Especially now," Jo reassured her sister. "I just need to stay here for a while until I can decide what it is that I want to do next."

"You know this is always your home, Jo, and whatever you decide, I'll always support you. Maybe you can take a few days to go swimming, boating, hiking... whatever it is you need to do to take your mind off everything and just relax until you figure out what you want to do. It's okay to take your time. We've all gone through some major transformations this year, but I believe that it will get better," Cora encouraged her sister, squeezing the hand she held once more.

Jo looked over and gave her sister another grateful smile. "So, Mom's birthday... Andrea told me that you wanted to continue the tradition that Dad started. What are your plans?" she asked, changing the subject.

"Oh, yeah, but I also want to make it better, you know— a huge family affair," Cora said.

Jo reached for the merlot and poured herself another drink.

Chapter Three

Jo felt the first rays of sun stream through her window and cast their shadow through her closed eyelids. She groaned as she slowly opened her eyes but quickly shut them from the intensity with which the beams fell on her retinas. Her head felt as though a million tiny balls were being volleyed back and forth in it. She felt sluggish as she tried to haul herself off her bed, and a wave of nausea suddenly hit her the minute she managed to stand to her feet. Jo hurriedly held on to the wall for support as she leaned slightly forward, willing the feeling away.

"Ugh, why did I drink so much wine?" she lamented after her nausea had subsided. Gingerly she made her way through her bedroom door and headed for the bathroom across from it. Jo splashed cold water on her face as she stood by the sink. She cast her gaze to the mirror behind the sink to look at her appearance. Her face was pallid, and there were circles under her eyes from how little sleep she got. Alcohol and insomnia were not a good mix.

She would have to make something that could alleviate the

queasiness in her stomach and go for a run to get her heart rate up and her blood pumping to rid herself of the remaining toxins from the wine and the fatigue her body was feeling.

After taking a quick shower, she put on her running gear and headed downstairs.

The rich aroma of fermented yeast, burnt sugar, and cinnamon wafted to her nostrils before she even entered the kitchen. She wondered if either of her sisters had actually gotten up before her.

"Morning, Mom. You're up early," she greeted Becky, surprised to find her sitting at the kitchen island with a cup of coffee and two baskets of freshly baked croissants and cinnamon rolls.

Her mother looked over and gave her a warm smile. "Good morning, sweetie. I'm usually up by this time so that I can get some crocheting done."

Jo looked down at her mother's hands to see her holding a beautiful, multicolored, patterned piece in one hand while her other fed intricate loops with a needle to the continued growth of the piece.

"Wow, Mom. I didn't know you crocheted," Jo spoke, surprised as she reached for a mug from the cabinet above the sink. She then reached over to turn on the kettle.

"I've always loved crocheting and knitting," Becky informed her. "I just didn't get around to doing it until recently." She put the needle down to take a sip of the coffee that sat on the table beside her. "Plus, it helps in keeping my hands steady," she finished.

Jo nodded her understanding and pushed away from the sink to get a lemon and ginger from the refrigerator.

"That's great, Mom. I'm happy you have something that keeps you occupied and helps with the other thing," she expressed, not comfortable enough to address her mother's illness by name. It felt as if it would become even more real than it already was, and she wasn't prepared to deal with what that truly meant.

After adding the ginger and a squeeze of lemon juice to the hot water she'd poured into the mug, she sweetened the mixture with honey before taking a few sips. She'd loved this remedy. It had always brought relief when she'd had a little too much alcohol. She sat on a stool at the island across from her mother and chanced taking a freshly baked croissant from the basket, praying that it wouldn't cause her stomach further unease.

"So why are you up so early?" Becky asked, starting up the conversation once more.

"I couldn't sleep," Jo answered, bringing the hot liquid to her lips. "I think I drank a little too much last night."

Her mother's brown eyes looked over at her with understanding, but she also noticed the look of concern in them as well.

"I got comfortable... too comfortable it seems, and I drank a little bit more than I normally would. It isn't something I practice," she rushed to further explain and hopefully alleviate her mother's worry and questions.

Becky nodded. "So, how is my lovely granddaughter doing?" she asked as if sensing it would be better to keep the questions away from delving to much into her daughter's own well-being.

"Tracy's great. She's finally starting college in the fall, and she and Josh are doing really well," Jo expressed with a small smile of relief.

"That's wonderful, sweetie," her mother said, pleased. "Have they set a date?"

"No, not yet," Jo answered. "I just know it won't be this year because Tracy wants to focus on her studies, seeing that she didn't start when she was supposed to," she continued to explain.

Becky nodded. "There's no rush. They're still young, and they have a lifetime to do it right."

"That's true," Jo agreed, taking a bite of the bread and reveling in the crisp, slightly sweet and savory taste. "Mmm, this is really good, Mom," she gushed. "There's something in this that I have never tasted before. It is so distinct, but I can't put my finger on it," she murmured in thought.

"Thank you, sweetie. It's my own special touch," Becky informed her.

"You have got to teach me the recipe and all the others you've kept to yourself all these years," Jo requested.

"When the time is right," Becky replied with a twinkle in her dark brown eyes, which only her youngest daughter had inherited.

Jo raised the cup to her lips and took a sip before responding, "I will hold you to that, Mom."

Becky stared back at her daughter, a small smile embedded on her lips.

"What?" Jo asked, disconcerted by her mother's unwavering gaze. She could see the sadness, the regret behind those dark brown irises.

"I'm just happy that you're here," Becky simply stated.

Jo gave her mother a tight-lipped smile, aware of the double meaning of her mother's statement. "I think I'm going to go for a run and get some fresh air," she announced, pushing away from the island to bring her cup to the sink and wash.

Becky didn't say anything but continued to stare at her daughter's back with saddened eyes. When Jo turned back to her, she quickly plastered on a small smile. "Are you sure you don't want to wait for Cora? She usually goes for a run around this time as well; maybe she'll be down in a bit," she reasoned with her.

A look of uncertainty flashed through Jo's eyes before she

declined. "No, that's fine, Mom. I really just need some time to clear my head and get in a few miles by myself."

Becky nodded in understanding. "Okay, sweetie, be safe out there."

"I will, thanks." With that, Jo headed for the front door, ran down the three short porch steps, and took off for the road that would lead her off the property and onto the highway.

A half hour into her run, Jo felt the tension finally start to leave her body and mind as her breathing became less labored and the fast beating of her heart decreased to an even tempo. Her focus was now taken to her surroundings as her feet took her past the Oak Harbor Marina and the city's main strip on SE Pioneer Way toward Windjammer Park. She ran past the baseball fields, the basketball courts, and splash park, past undefined open fields, and made her way toward the beach.

The moment her sneaker-clad feet hit the sand, which formed the perfect boundary between the park and the water, Jo slowed her pace until she came to a full stop. The sun was now much higher and brighter against the cloudless, light blue sky that intersected the blue waters of the pacific extending for miles. The slight wind brought with it the fresh smell of salt that tickled her nostrils.

The picturesque view before her, coupled with her run, had effectively taken her mind off the radiating hole of sorrow that was permanently lodged in her chest since the loss of Charles and Nicholas. Just being out in the open and away from everyone gave her clarity, peace, and an escape from the reality she now lived in for a while. In the past year, running had become a major part of her daily routine— it gave her time to reset.

As she looked out across the horizon, Cora's words from last night seeped into her mind. She knew that this would always be her home. If she was honest with herself, she knew it always had been. Still, with all the bad memories that came with it and the loss of her estranged father, who she had thought still resented his daughters for abandoning the path he had chosen for them to pursue their own up until recently, she wasn't sure it was a wise idea to provide more opportunity for the hole in her chest to widen even more. There were just too many regrets, too many unspoken apologies, and missed opportunities to remind her that this was yet again one more area she would not get full closure from.

She wrapped her hands around her torso as a wave of sadness chilled her. Perhaps this had been a mistake from the beginning, as she had originally thought.

"I'll give it until Mom's birthday then if it still doesn't feel right... I'll figure something out," she reasoned with herself.

She turned and made her way toward the park, preparing to start her run home when she exited. As she ran along the marina, she made a mental note to visit the fish market to get some deep-water catches. The chef in her raved at the thought of buying and preparing some of the freshest seafood that one could ever get in the Continental US. She made a note to revisit for that sole purpose. As she made her way toward Maui Avenue, she noticed another jogger not too far from her heading in the opposite direction. The woman's eyes were laser-focused on her and made her self-conscious. Even after they passed each other, she could feel her gaze boring a hole in the back of her head.

"Jo!"

Jo's steps faltered as she turned to look back at the stranger that had just called her name, but the closer she came, the more recognizable she became. The woman removed the knitted hat on her head to reveal her auburn-colored hair pulled back in a low bun. Her facial features hadn't changed that much over the past twenty or so years either. Apart from filling out and a few laugh lines around her mouth and eyes, she was the same, just an older version.

"I can't believe you passed me like that. Like we didn't just see each other a few months back. I know it was brief with you jetting off after the funeral, but still..." the woman spoke in a hurtful tone even though her eyes glinted with mischief.

"Kerry." Jo broke out in a huge grin as her cousin stepped up and placed her arms around her in a warm embrace.

"I'm so glad you came home, Jo," Kerry whispered with relief against her shoulder.

Jo's smile wavered.

Chapter Four

"So, how is that beautiful daughter of yours?" Kerry asked Jo as they stood along the side of the road conversing. "I know I only saw her that one time but boy, is she the spitting image of you when you were that age and equally as beautiful if not more."

At her cousin's compliment, Jo couldn't help but feel the warmth that colored her cheeks. "Look who's talking," she deflected, "Miss, I haven't aged a day over twenty-five in the last sixteen years."

It was Kerry's time to blush profusely before a wide grin graced her lips.

"Gosh, I've missed you, Jo," Kerry spoke sincerely as her sapphire blue eyes glimmered.

"I've missed you too, Kerry Bear," Jo returned, using the nickname she'd given her cousin so long ago as an endearment.

Kerry grinned once more. "So back on topic," she reminded Jo.

"Oh yes, Tracy is fine, fantastic. She's starting college soon and engaged to a wonderful young man."

"That is so great to hear. I'm happy for you, Jo." Kerry smiled. "So, are they planning on having the wedding here?"

Jo contemplated the woman's question. "No. They haven't chosen a venue just yet. They've just been so busy," she revealed.

"Okay, well, if they choose to do it here, consider my services of providing the wedding cake free of charge. My treat," Kerry offered.

"Oh, that's right. Cora told me you have your own bakery. That's really generous of you, Kerry," Jo said.

"No problem at all, and yes," Kerry beamed with pride. "I opened the shop after my divorce," she continued to say.

"I'm happy for you, Kerry. I know this was your dream back in high school. It's good to see you finally have what you've always wanted," Jo congratulated the woman, still beaming with pride.

"If you think that's great, then you should see what Dee's up to," Kerry added.

Jo racked her brain, trying to figure out who Dee was.

"That's Dianne, Tessa's daughter," Kerry clarified.

"Oh," she replied simply.

"She's celebrating the first-year anniversary of her business Java Bistro, and she's setting up a kiosk at the Whidbey Island Fair tomorrow. You should come," she invited.

"I didn't know there was a fair in town," Jo replied, surprised that she hadn't been aware.

"Yeah, they've been here about a week now and will be until the end of summer. But seriously you should come tomorrow. It'll be fun," Kerry insisted.

Jo hesitated before speaking, "I'll think about it," she appeased her cousin.

"Good," Kerry returned, satisfied.

After the two parted, Jo finally made her way home.

"Hey, Sis. How was your run?" Andrea sat on the porch, sporting reading glasses with her laptop opened on her lap.

"Hey," Jo greeted, coming to rest her back on the railing before her sister. "It was good. Guess who I ran into?"

Her sister's bright blue eyes stared up at her quizzically. "Who?" she asked.

"You're supposed to guess," Jo deadpanned.

"Jo, you know I don't have the patience for those things." Andrea chuckled. Jo couldn't help but join in.

"Kerry," she revealed after her laughter had died down. "She invited me to the Whidbey Island Fair tomorrow. She said Tessa's daughter, Dianne, is testing the market for her new kiosk idea."

"Oh, that's great. We should definitely go." She buzzed with excitement.

"Go where?"

Jo looked to the source of the voice to see Cora making her way up the steps, a wrapped tin foil container in her hands.

"The Whidbey Fair. Kerry invited Jo along to see Dianne's new kiosk idea, and I thought we should tag along," Andrea offered up.

"Oh, I saw the flier and drove past there a few times. We should definitely go," she readily agreed. "I haven't been to a fair in years.

"What's that?" Jo jutted her chin toward the container in her hand.

"Oh, this is a chicken lasagna for dinner, courtesy of Chef Daniel," she answered. "Let me just go pop this in the refrigerator. I'll be back."

"So, what're you doing?" Jo turned to Andrea, pointing at the laptop she had.

"I'm creating a website for the fire department."

Jo looked at her sister questioningly.

"It's a really long and weird story, but yeah, I agreed to create the website for the department." Andrea expressed.

Jo nodded in understanding. As far as she was aware, her sister never steered toward this path in her field of work.

"Okay," she replied simply, keeping back what she wanted to ask for another time.

* * *

A kaleidoscope of colors painted the darkened skies with their brilliance; the different rides of attraction stood looming and inviting the adventurous to come to take a chance at being catapulted or suspended in the air, defying the laws of gravity. The enormous Ferris wheel stood at the center of it, all lit up like a gateway to another universe.

As Jo and her sisters continued to walk around, taking in everything, the energy and vibrancy of the fairground left the air buzzing as screams of excitement competed with the booming music playing and announcers using megaphones to invite patrons to their booths to try their luck or simply buy something special. It was all chaotic, and yet it came together so well.

Her sense of smell was also bombarded with a myriad of aromas that sent her senses into overdrive. She smelled hot dogs, hamburgers, the sweetness of cotton candy, caramel apples, and every other scent that she couldn't readily identify but also assaulted her senses.

"Where did Kerry say we should meet her again?" Cora called out above the noise.

"She said Dianne's kiosk will be closer to the carousel," Jo replied, pointing to the huge structure rotating on its axis as children and adults wore fringe smiles, giggled, and squealed as the horses who moved up and down made 360-degree rotations.

The sisters walked toward the contraption, keeping their eyes out for the booth where their cousins would be.

"There it is." Cora gestured toward the sign that read, "Java Bistro."

The three hurriedly made their way toward the booth, where they could see their auburn-haired cousin speaking animatedly and laughing with a young woman with chestnut-colored hair that lay just above her shoulder blades in a sleek bob.

"Kerry," Jo elevated her voice above the music and other sounds to get her cousin's attention.

Kerry turned to them, and a large grin decorated her face before she rushed from behind the booth to come to hug each sister.

"I'm so glad you guys made it," she said gratefully.

Jo gave her a light smile.

"Come meet Dee," she invited, speaking specifically to Jo, who had not met Dianne officially yet.

"Dee, this is Jo," she introduced.

The young lady smiled politely at her and held out her hand for a handshake.

"It's nice to meet you," the young woman spoke.

Jo squeezed her hand in greeting. "The pleasure is all mine. Happy one-year anniversary on your business. So, this is the kiosk." She turned toward the glass display that showcased different cuts of meat for sandwiches and bread and condiments. There was also a section of the glass display taken up by the cakes and other pastries.

"Yes," Dianne confirmed, although it was not needed.

"It's lovely. I like it."

At this, Dianne gave her a grateful smile.

"Let's go have some fun," she heard her oldest sister say, then Andrea and Kerry agreed.

"Go. I'll be okay until you get back," Dianne told her aunt, who had been worried about leaving her alone.

The four women set out to walk around the fairgrounds to catch up and have some fun.

"I want to go on the Ferris wheel so bad," Andrea said in a childlike voice which caused her to snicker. Looking over at her sister, she noted the wistful look in her own eyes as she looked up at the structure making its rotation.

"Let's go," Jo called out as she grabbed her sister's hand and pulled her to the line of eagerly waiting patrons.

Cora and Kerry came up behind them, chatting and laughing.

When they finally made it to the front of the line, they were strapped into their seats two by two, Cora with Kerry and Jo with Andrea.

Jo felt exhilarated as the cart she was in lifted off the ground and into the air as more people were directed into their seats. Slowly the wheel began to turn, and gradually the speed increased. From that vantage point, Jo bet she could see all the way across the Pacific up to Canada if time weren't so dark now.

When they finally made it back to the ground, her feet were wobbly, and she felt as if she had a bad case of motion sickness— still, she felt as though she could go again.

"Let's try the bulls-eye," Andrea suggested that they do that next.

The women agreed and made their way toward the booth, but just then, someone called out to them.

"Hey, Triple H!"

Jo turned to the voices and saw a group of five men approaching them. A few of them looked vaguely familiar, but there were a few she was sure she had no clue who they were.

"Jack," she heard Andrea greet the bald-headed man with enough bulk to make him a bouncer or a bodyguard as he gave her a light hug. She remembered Jack. He'd been a close friend of her sisters, and she had run in the same circle when she finally made it to high school. She also remembered she had met him at the bar he now owned.

"It's so good to see you," Cora said as she, too, went in for a hug.

"So, what about me?" a deep baritone voice asked.

"Jeremy," Cora cheesed. "I can't believe it's really you."

"In the flesh," the man returned with a huge smile.

She remembered Jeremy. He'd been one of Cora's closest friends back in high school, but then life had happened, and everyone had gone their separate ways.

"Jo," she heard her name being called. Looking over, she noticed the gentleman with jet-black hair and moss-colored eyes staring at her expectantly.

Suddenly recognition sparked. "Gary," she spoke almost disbelievingly. "I can't believe you're here... in Oak Harbor," she said honestly as the man brought her into a tight embrace. Gary had been her high school sweetheart but had broken up with her in their senior year because he was migrating to France. She'd never in a million years thought she would ever see him again, but here he was in the flesh and just as handsome and larger than life as he had always been.

"It is good to see you, Jo," he said sincerely as he held her at arms-length. "You haven't changed one bit," he complimented.

At this, Jo playfully slapped him in the chest. "Oh, stop lying, Gary," she returned half-jokingly, half seriously.

"It's the truth, Jo," he reiterated, his green eyes holding hers, reflecting his sincerity.

"You haven't changed that much yourself," she said, giving him another smile. The two finally separated.

"So, you live here now?" she asked, mildly curious.

"No, actually. I'm just passing through. I live in Italy now. My wife and daughter are there," he explained.

"Oh, that's wonderful, Gary. I'm happy for you," she congratulated, truly happy for him.

"Thanks, Jo," he returned her smile. "Oh, this is my friend Daniel Pierce," he said, turning to a man that stood behind him with his hands in his pocket. His dark hair that was slightly slicked back sat above his high forehead and went well with his high cheekbones and sharp jawline. That and his very lean physique gave him a youthful appearance. If it weren't for the strands of gray hair at his temples, she might have mistaken him for being in his mid-to-late thirties. One other thing that truly caught her attention was how tall he was. He seemed to be over six feet tall. She also had a distinct feeling that she had met him somewhere.

"But you probably already knew that, seeing that he's the chef at Willberry Eats."

Jo widened her eyes in surprise.

Chapter Five

"Hi, I don't think we've formally met, but it's a pleasure." Jo held her hand out to the gentleman whose light pink lips turned upward into a welcoming smile as he reached for her hand.

"The pleasure is all mine, Ms. Hamilton." His voice was deep yet gentle with a tinge of an accent. He raised her hand to his lip and lightly kissed her flesh, surprising Jo.

"Please call me Jo, short for Josephine. I prefer that," she implored him as the shock of the moment receded.

The man gave her a slight nod of acceptance.

"I take it you're not from around here?" she asked with a raised brow.

Daniel chuckled, an action that seemed to incorporate his whole body as the sound reverberated from his chest, making his shoulders move up and down.

"What gave it away?" he asked in a playful tone.

"Well, for one, the fact that you have an accent, and two, your way of greeting isn't very American," she stated matter-of-factly.

At this, the man laughed, giving Jo the perfect view of his Adam's apple bobbing with the movement as his head leaned backward, exposing his neck. She quickly averted her eyes and waited for him to finish.

"I suppose your observation is spot on, although a bit unconventional and lacking in facts," he gave in when he had settled down.

"Really? How so?" Jo asked, raising a brow in challenge.

"Well, for one..." he started, his steel-gray eyes glimmering with laughter under the fair's flickering lights and a smirk gracing his lips, "I was born in America at Whidbey Health Center, to be exact. However, my father, who is French decided to move his family back to France when I was only one year old. French became my official language for some time. Number two, my parents taught me the true meaning of commentaire être un gentleman."

"What did you say at the end?" she asked, intrigued.

"I said, they taught me how to be a gentleman," he revealed.

"I suppose on that premise, all of my assumptions were incorrect then." Jo sighed in mock defeat, drawing another laugh from Daniel.

"You are interesting," he commented, which brought a smile of uncertainty to Jo's lips.

"So, how do you know Gary?" she asked, changing the subject.

"He hit me with his car and sent me to the hospital for nearly a month," Daniel replied nonchalantly.

"He what?" Jo half shrieked. She looked over at Gary talking animatedly with her sisters and cousin and the other men that had joined the group.

"It wasn't his fault."

Jo looked up at the giant of a man that made her five-four height look like a dwarf and waited for him to expound.

"It happened in France, in Cannes to be exact. I was on my

way to get fresh produce for the upcoming special at L'éponyme..." He paused as if noticing Jo's look of confusion. "L'éponyme is the name of the restaurant that I worked for as chef de cuisine."

This term Jo was familiar with.

"I was not looking where I was going, or rather, I was too focused on getting to the market on the other side of the street that I did not see the car traveling in the wrong direction hurtling toward me. By the time I did, it had already hit me and run over my leg. In Gary's defense, he hadn't known it was a one-way street, and I had already stepped before the car."

"I'm so sorry to hear that," Jo replied, barely audible as she wrapped her hand around her waist, shivering from the memory of the two accidents that claimed her loved ones.

Daniel, as if sensing the shift in her mood, quickly spoke up. "Don't worry about it. It was more than twenty years ago, and after spending just a month in the hospital, we became almost inseparable. He was like the annoying little brother I never had."

At this, a grin graced Jo's lips at his description of Gary. "That seems like a harsh thing to call a grown man," she mused.

Daniel went to answer her when she heard her name being called, "Jo!"

She swiveled her head to look back at her sisters. Cora held her cell to her ear while she beckoned her to come over. Giving Daniel an apologetic smile, she made her way over to the group as he followed close behind.

"What's up?" she asked Andrea as soon as she was in hearing range.

"We're going down to Double Bluff Beach. Do you wanna come? Oh, hi, Chef," her sister rushed out. Daniel flashed a smile in greeting.

"At this hour?" Jo asked skeptically, looking down at her watch.

"Oh, come on, Jo. Lighten up a bit. It's just after nine p.m. It's just for a bit of fun and relaxation," Andrea implored her sister. "It's going to be fun," she pushed at the sign of Jo's reluctance. "Plus, Cora's boyfriend"—she emphasized with air quotes— "is on his way here to join us." She wiggled her eyebrows suggestively.

Jo laughed at her sister's antics. "Okay, fine. I'm in," she agreed more out of curiosity to see the dynamics between her sister and the contractor she had started dating than it was to be out in the night air reminiscing on old high school memories. "But please don't do that eye thing again," she warned her sister.

"Yay!" Andrea squealed in joy.

Taking the phone from her ear, Cora came to stand before her sisters. "Jamie said he'd be here in the next ten minutes," she announced.

Jo could see that her sister was becoming enamored with the man if the slight breathiness of her voice or the deepening redness of her cheeks that had nothing to do with the somewhat chilly night were anything to go by. She was happy for her. After everything Joel had done to her, she deserved to be happy.

Her mind flashed back to a bit of news that had completely rocked her off-center and made her question what was true and what was a mirage of perfectly packed lies.

"Are you okay?" Andrea bumped her shoulder as she looked at her worriedly.

Jo quickly plastered on a smile. "Yes, of course. I just got sidetracked for a minute," she answered.

At this, Andrea gave her an understanding smile before putting an arm around her shoulder and bringing her close to her side. Jo warmed over at the action, grateful that her sister always knew how to make her feel better even without the use of words. It had always been like that between them, and even after leaving Oak Harbor to start their separate lives, she had always been able to call upon Andrea to help push her through her rough patches.

"I'm glad you're here," her sister whispered against her hair, bringing a small smile to her face. Jo reached over to pat the hand on her upper arm in gratitude.

Just then, Kerry stepped back into the circle. "I invited Dee to come with us, but she was like, no, it's okay. Go spend time with people your age. I don't mind. Like what is that?" she asked in an offended tone, drawing laughs from those who had heard her rant. "Why are you all laughing? A twenty-five-year-old just called the lot of you old, geriatric," she continued dramatically.

"Oh, lighten up, Kerry. It's not like we're running in the same circles as these millennials," Jack tried to reason with her.

"Yeah, well, wait until yours start calling you old man, and then tell me how it feels," she rebutted.

Jo couldn't help the laugh that left her lips at how melodramatic Kerry was being. She truly hadn't changed.

Just then, a very tall man, she guessed he had to be the same height as Daniel, came toward their group. He had glistening black hair with a touch of gray at his temples and a peppered goatee that framed his oval face. The T-shirt he wore displayed the broad expanse of a hard chest, and the short sleeves exposed his muscled arms. He walked with purpose until he stood right behind Cora, who had been talking to Malachi, another one of their high school mates. He lightly tapped her shoulder, and Cora turned her head to look at him. Jo witnessed the moment her sister's mannerisms changed. A deep rosy flush covered her cheeks, and a bashful smile graced her lips as she excused herself from the conversation she was having to turn fully to the man. She noticed when Jamie reached out his hand to lightly brush his fingers against her forearm. If she could get closer without being intrusive, Jo was certain she would have seen the tiny goose bumps trailing down her arm.

"Cute, right?" her sister asked, interrupting her thoughts.

"They are," she agreed.

Shortly after Jamie's arrival, everyone piled into their own vehicles, and they all made their way over to Double Bluff Beach off Route 525. Cora had chosen to drive with Jamie, which left Andrea and Jo in her Jeep.

The group followed the darkened path, slightly illuminated by the moonlight above. Jo could hear the splash of waves against the shore in the distance. Soon enough, her sandal-clad feet scrunched against the sandy shore as she followed the group.

When they were a good distance along the beach, the men gathered driftwood, piling them up to make a bonfire. Jo readily took a seat on one of the tree stumps that had been organized in a circle around the fire. She eagerly held her hands out in front of the flames, enjoying the heat that traveled up her arms.

She watched, mesmerized as the yellow flames swayed at the beckoning of the wind as sparks of fire separated themselves to shoot up into the dark sky like small flamboyant fireflies.

She suddenly felt someone sit beside her on the log. Looking over, she was met with the smiling face of Daniel. "Hi."

"Hi." Jo gave him a small grin.

"I thought you'd like one," he offered her an unopened can of beer which she gladly took from him.

"Thanks."

The two sat in comfortable silence while the others drank and chatted animatedly around the fire or were splashing about in the warm ocean. She looked across the fire to see her sister snuggled up to Jamie, who had his arm around her shoulder as she rested her back against his chest.

"So, how long have you been back in Whidbey, Oak Harbor to be specific?" she turned to ask Daniel.

It took the man some time to answer her question, making her question whether it had been a good idea to perpetuate the serenity of the moment by talking.

"I moved back here nearly twenty years ago," he finally spoke. "I came here with my wife and three-year-old daughter, but sadly, only one of those two relationships has remained intact."

Jo waited for him to continue. Daniel looked over at her before quickly averting his eyes. "I'm divorced."

"I'm sorry to hear that," Jo replied, unsure of what else she could have said in such a situation.

"So, your mother tells me you're a chef," he changed the conversation.

Jo blinked, surprised her mother had spoken to him about her. "Oh, yeah... yes. Sous chef actually," she informed him.

"What was it like working in the city?" he asked, interested.

"Busy." She laughed. "It was great, actually. I've always loved being in the kitchen, and the opportunity I had to be second in command at such an upscale restaurant was just..." She couldn't find the words to express her feelings. "I also did a little catering on the side, so when I say I was busy, I mean I was almost wrung out."

"Sounds remarkable," Daniel countered. "I hope I'm not making a conclusion based on a false assumption here, but seeing as you're here, back in Oak Harbor, maybe you could help me prepare for your mother's sixty-sixth birthday party coming up," he offered.

"Really?" she asked wide-eyed. "Of course. I would love to, and I promise I won't get in your way." She gave her scout's honor. At this, Daniel chuckled heartily.

"What's so funny over here?" Andrea asked as she plopped down on the other side of Jo.

"Daniel was just asking me to assist him with making Mom's birthday dinner," Jo told her sister.

"That's great," Andrea replied, pleased.

"Cora," Andrea called out to her sister, grabbing her attention. "Jo's gonna help prepare Mom's birthday dinner."

"That's great news," Cora replied, disentangling herself from Jamie, then headed over to her sisters.

"I'm sure Mom will appreciate it even more." Cora smiled down at her baby sister in appreciation. Jo returned her smile.

"And what about me?"

The sisters turned to their cousin, who stood looking back and forth between them in expectation.

"Thank you for agreeing to take time out of your busy schedule to make and decorate Mom's cake, Kerry," Cora appeased their cousin.

"Aww, shucks, you're going to make me cry."

Cora chuckled before pulling her into a hug.

"Now that that's settled, we need to make sure that our girls show up for this party because... it might just be Mom's last," Andrea spoke solemnly.

Jo felt her heart constrict with dread, and the hole in her chest widen a little more.

Chapter Six

Four days later

"Do you remember this one?"

Jo looked over at the photo Andrea had pulled from the family album as they sat in the wicker chairs on the east side of the wraparound porch overlooking the water.

"Oh my God... how did that even make it in there?" Jo asked, mortified.

"Let me see," Cora called from beside her. Her sister snickered the moment she passed the photo over to her. "Look at those rosy cheeks," she gushed, looking over at Jo with puppy dog eyes.

Jo sucked her teeth, reaching for the photo.

Cora leaned away from her sister's hand. "Look, Drea, it's Jo, the diver," she joked, waving the photo in Andrea's direction.

At this, Andrea cackled while Jo settled back in her seat with her arms folded across her chest, huffing. She chose to ignore her two annoying siblings and instead focused her attention on the dark blue waters. She could see the small ripples within the still tranquility. The birds soared high in the bright blue sky as the yellow sun beat down on the water's surface. It all looked like a picture from a postcard. It was so beautiful. She loved all of it.

"All right, Jo, we're sorry. Here you go," Cora broke into her thoughts, handing the picture back to her.

She took it from her sister and looked down at it with a frown. The picture had been one of the worst and most embarrassing days of her life. She ran track back in high school, and on the day in question, they had a meet back at the old sports center in Harbor Heights. The track had lines sprayed onto the grassy field, and rain had fallen just over an hour before she was slated to race. She had been confident of a victory, having gone into the two hundred meters as the favorite to win, but just thirty meters away from her victory, she buckled and went sliding over the wet grass, taking down two other runners with her. In the end, she was disqualified, and the race was not run over, leaving many people angry and disappointed with her, especially the two runners she had tripped. As she looked down at the photo that one of her friends had snapped with his camera and given her a printout, much to her chagrin, she couldn't help but wonder why her father had chosen to keep that photo. Sure, there were others in the album showcasing her many wins, both academically and athletically.

Flipping the photo over, she noticed the writing at the bottom, *"a reminder that failure is not permanent. Dad."* It brought a smile to her lips.

"Are you okay?"

Jo turned her head to the side to see Cora giving her an anxious look.

"Mmmhmm," she replied. "I was just thinking about Dad," she continued, "and how he never gave up on this place or that one day we would come back, albeit it had to take his life for it to happen."

"Dad was a proud man, Jo. He didn't know how to admit that he was sorry, and neither did we," Andrea spoke up. She paused and looked out at the water, and Jo waited for her to continue. "I feel like I owe it to him, Mom, and myself to make sure that this place carries on the legacy that he put so much of his time and energy into building for his family, for all of us." At her last statement, Andrea looked over at her sisters with much feeling.

"Yes," Cora chimed in. "I believe so too, Drea."

Jo simply nodded in agreement as the three settled into a comfortable silence.

"I like the colors you chose for the inn's interior, Drea. They really brighten the place and give it a welcoming kind of vibe," Jo complimented her sister, who had taken on the responsibility of redecorating the inn.

"Oh yeah? You think so?" Andrea asked, pleased by her sister's approval.

"Yeah. I mean, I know it's not finished yet, but from what I saw and the discussions I had with Marg about the type of furniture you're planning to add to the foyer and sitting area, I can't wait to see how it turns out."

"See, Cora, it's not even finished yet, and already the compliments are coming in. Marg said a few of the guests also commented on how much they loved the colors downstairs and that they hoped we would be continuing with the guest rooms as well. I told you it was a good idea."

At this, Cora chuckled lightly, "Okay, Drea. Your idea was a winning one."

"So, are there any more plans for renovations or upgrades?" Jo asked.

"Oh, yes. Dad left a ton of things that he wanted to be done. Jamie has completed most of them so far, like the gazebo at the back of the inn, the dock that was raised, a firewood house, and the upgraded rose garden," Cora informed her.

"Wow, that's a lot," Jo mused. "What about the restaurant?"

"Well, nothing more has been done to the space. Maybe you could take a look and make it a project of your own," Cora suggested.

Jo hesitated to answer. She wasn't even sure how long she was actually planning on staying there. Her mother's birthday was just around the corner, and she had given herself until then to make her decision.

"Yeah, maybe," she answered noncommittally. Andrea and Cora exchanged a look between them that didn't go unnoticed by her. "Where did you say Mom went again?" she asked, choosing not to comment on the incident.

"She said she was going over to Mrs. Borden's to play cribbage with a few of her old friends," Andrea informed her.

"Do you think it's a wise idea for her to be out and about by herself like that?" Jo asked, truly worried.

"Relax, Jo," Cora stepped in. "This is something she has been doing for a very long time. She can't just stop living because of this illness."

Jo sighed exasperatedly. "That's not what I meant, Cora. It's just... I don't know. I'm just worried that something could happen to her, and none of us are there for her." Jo turned her head away from her sister's probing blue eyes to look out across the horizon once more. She knew she was being irrational, but with the death of her husband, her son, and her father, she couldn't help the paranoia or the doomsday thinking that popped up on occasion from the fear now deeply embedded of losing her loved ones without warning at any instant.

She felt a hand on her shoulder before it rubbed it in circles. "She's fine, Jo," Cora spoke soothingly. "Nothing is going to happen. We're all here to make sure of it, but we have to give her space to breathe and feel normal. If we take that away from her, we'll set her up to start worrying more, and we would have lost her even before the sickness was able to do its damage," she continued to reason.

"She'll be fine, Jo," Andrea added as she reached out and held her sister's hand reassuringly.

"I know..." Jo replied. "Thanks."

The sisters gave her smiles of assurance.

Just then, the doorbell sounded from inside.

"I'll get it," Cora offered, jumping to her feet and heading for the side door that led straight into the kitchen.

"Hey, are you okay?" Andrea asked, worried lines etched on her face.

"I am," Jo confirmed. "It's just sometimes... well lately... I have been overthinking everything."

Andrea gave her an understanding look. "Just remember I'm always here to talk, Jo," she offered. "And when it feels like it's too much, I'll make you popcorn with a ton of butter, then I'll put on a sappy comedy so that you can laugh until the tears run down your cheeks— no judgment of course, and then I'll let eat your buttery treat to your heart's content."

Jo reached over to squeeze her sister's hand. "I'm so happy that I have a sister like you," she spoke with feeling. Andrea returned her squeeze.

Just then, Cora walked out with a gentleman Jo had never met before. His blond hair was much taller than a buzz cut and was tapered at the sides, with a few of the longer strands falling over his forehead that displayed a set of blue eyes, a straight nose, and thin pink lips. From where she sat, she assumed he had to be at least five ten, and he looked very athletic.

She noticed Andrea's eyes widened in surprise when she looked up and saw him.

"Donny, what are you doing here?" Andrea asked, her voice an octave higher than normal.

"Hi, Drea. I'm sorry to intrude like this, but something went wrong with the website, and people have been calling and saying they're not able to view the information under the drop-down sections. I was wondering if you could have a look. I should have called, but I was coming this way, so I just decided to stop by instead."

Andrea stood to her feet and smoothed down the sides of her flared skirt. "No, that's fine. I'm glad you came. I mean, I'm happy to be of assistance."

Jo marveled at how flustered her sister, who was always so together and sure of herself, seemed to be. Interesting, she thought.

"Hi," the man, just noticing Jo staring at them, greeted.

"Oh, I forgot you haven't met my sister, Josephine. Jo, this is Donny Hasgrove. He's the lieutenant at the Oak Harbor Fire Department," Andrea introduced the two.

"It's a pleasure to meet you, Mr. Hasgrove," Jo said as she took the hand stretched out to her.

"The pleasure is all mine, and please just call me Donny. That's fine."

Jo gave him a polite smile. "Then please just call me Jo. Everyone else does," she offered.

"Okay, Jo. It's nice to meet you again." With that, he turned back to Andrea, who looked anxious by their exchange.

"I was hoping you could come by the station to fix it," he told her.

"Yes, of course. Let me just get my sandals, and we can go. It's by the door so just follow me." Andrea turned to her sisters. "See you guys later."

"Ladies." Donny slightly bowed in parting.

When the two disappeared into the house, Jo turned to

Cora. "So, you didn't tell me Andrea also had a love interest," she spoke accusingly.

"They're just friends," Cora returned. "But by the rate of things, I bet it will be more than that by the end of the month," Cora continued, nodding suggestively.

"That's nice," Jo said, and she meant it. She was happy to know that there was a possibility that her sister, who had given up on love for umpteen years now, could possibly be giving it another go. She was happy and prayed that Andrea would hold on to it.

Cora's phone rang, bringing her out of her thoughts.

"It's Jules," Cora revealed, happily bringing the phone to her ear. "Hi, sweetie. How are you? Wait, slow down, Jules. Mm-hmm, uh-huh.... You're what?"

At Cora's last statement, Jo whipped her head around to look at her sister, whose face had gone white as if she'd seen a ghost. The hand that held the phone lowered to her side, and then the device slipped through her fingers.

"Cora," Jo called out worriedly to her sister. "What's wrong?"

Cora looked up at her sister, her pain reflected in her eyes. "It's... it's... Jules thinks she's pregnant."

Chapter Seven

Jo bent down and picked up the phone her sister had dropped to the floor from the shock of the news. "Hello? Hi, Jules... Yes, it's Aunt Jo... Yes, she's still here. Hold on."

Jo held out the phone to her sister, who looked from it to her, eyes squinted in confusion.

"Jules is still on the phone. You need to speak to her, Cora. I know it's hard to hear such news, but this is the time she'll need you more than anything. She'll need your support so she doesn't make any more bad decisions that might make the situation even worse," she reasoned with her sister.

After another pause and Cora looking down at the phone as if it was a weapon, she finally scooped it out of Jo's hand and placed it by her ear.

"Hi, sweetie... no, I'm still here. You don't start school until September, so this is what I want you to do, Jules. Book a ticket back to Seattle and then take the ferry to the island. I'll come to pick you up when you get there... and honey... it's okay. Everything will be okay. I'm here for you, and we'll make it through this. Okay?"

After Cora hung up with her daughter, then slumped into the nearest chair, feeling defeated. Jo pulled up a chair to sit before her.

"How're you feeling?" Jo asked, rubbing her knee soothingly.

"Like I just got ran over by a train." Cora sighed, dejected.

"I know it's hard, possibly maddening, to know that your twenty-year-old daughter is possibly pregnant, but you have to think about how she is feeling now. You have to be there for her more than ever. The good thing is that you now have me, Drea and Mom, and the rest of the family to be there for you and Jules. It'll all work out. You know why?"

"Why?" Cora asked, drawn in.

"Because we're family, and family is everything. Besides with all that we have gone through and how it's affected us all this time, we owe it to ourselves and to our children not to mess up twice."

"Thanks, Jo," Cora replied sincerely. "I needed to hear that. I know everything will be fine because I have you and Andrea. I didn't realize how much I missed you two until recently and how I made it this far without you guys is truly a mystery to me now."

Jo gave her sister a bright smile. "The feeling is mutual, Cora." Reaching over, Cora pulled her into a hug.

* * *

"Ah, sweetie. You beat me this morning," Becky spoke, surprised to see her daughter in the kitchen with breakfast already prepared.

"I thought I'd surprise you for a change," Jo replied with a small smile. "Coffee?" she asked, moving toward the freshly brewed pot to pour her a cup.

"Thank you, sweetie." Becky gladly took the cup from her daughter, inhaling the rich aromatic steam rising from the cup. "Nothing like a fresh cup to get the day started right."

Jo nodded in agreement and turned to pour herself one. Jo brought the cup to her lips to take a sip of the hot liquid but almost spilled it and burned herself at the startling sound of glass shattering on the floor. She whipped around to see her mother's empty hand and wide, frightened eyes staring back at her.

"O-Oh... m-m-my... God... it just...fe-l-l."

Jo was shocked by the slurred words that came out in a thick heavy voice from her mother, along with the awkward curling of her fingers and her slightly shaking hand. In that instant, Jo came face to face with the tangibility of her mother's illness. She lifted her eyes to lock with her mother's, which were now registering the fear she felt in their brown orbs. Her eyes glistened as her tears pooled in them before a few slipped past their barrier to run down her cheeks.

"I-I'm... s-s-so... scared... swee-...tie."

Becky's revelation freed Jo from the shock, and she sprang into action, crossing to the other side of the island to engulf her mother's small, fragile frame in her embrace. "Shhh, it's okay, Mom," she soothed as Becky's tears began to fall even quicker, and her muffled sobs filled Jo's ears. "These things happen. It's just one of those days."

The words didn't carry as much weight as they normally would have. She knew that what she had just spoken to her mother was far from the reality she was in, and Becky knew it as well. "We'll get through this together. You, Cora, Andrea, and me," she changed her approach. "We're all here now, and we're not going anywhere." In that instant, she knew there was no way she could leave Oak Harbor again. Her mother needed her.

When the two separated, Jo offered, "Let me fix your breakfast and get you another cup of coffee, okay?"

"Thank you, Jo," Becky replied gratefully.

Jo realized that the slowed speech had receded and that her hand had stopped shaking and was now by her side. She was happy for that. Giving her mother another reassuring smile and ordering her to have a seat, Jo fixed her mother a plate of eggs, bacon, and some hash browns. She placed it before her, then her coffee. She then proceeded to clean up the glass chards on the floor and wiped up the liquid. Just as she took a seat in front of her own plate, the other three occupants in the house walked in.

"Mmm, it smells like a starving man's paradise. So delicious," Andrea commented, provoking a laugh from Jo and the others. "Looks heavenly too," she continued, looking at the platters of food set out and ready to be eaten.

"Those are the perks of having a chef for a sister," Cora added. "Thanks for making breakfast, Jo. Everything looks perfect." She turned to compliment her sister.

"You're welcome," Jo returned, looking from her two sisters to her niece. "Please have a seat. Mom and I..." Jo darted her gaze to her mother to see a look of worry on her face. "We just started eating. We just couldn't wait on you slowpokes to get down here."

The others sat and started piling their plates with food. The banter continued between the sisters for the duration of the meal, with Jo keeping a watchful eye on her mother, worried that a repeat of earlier could happen again. She knew her mother had been shaken up by what happened; she had been, too, but she also realized that it was not the news she wanted to share with the rest of the family, and she didn't want to embarrass her, so she kept the conversation light and funny to give her mother time to cope with what she was feeling.

"I need to tell you guys something."

At the somberness of Cora's voice, everyone at the island turned to her and waited with anticipation for her to continue.

"Umm, Jules called yesterday. She thinks... she thinks she might be pregnant."

There were audible gasps at the table after her announcement. Jo subtly shook her head in encouragement for Cora, who was looking at her, to continue.

"She should be arriving this week. I told her to book a flight to Seattle and then take the ferry, and I'll come to pick her up at Clinton."

"Oh, sweetie. I'm so sorry this is happening now," Becky spoke, reaching for her daughter's hand and giving it a comforting squeeze. Cora patted the hand she held in gratitude.

"We're all here for you, Cora, and for Jules. We'll get through this together," Andrea, who was beside her, spoke reassuringly, resting a hand on her shoulder.

"I know, and I'm grateful for all of you," Cora replied, giving her family a smile of appreciation. Aurora reached across the island to offer her own support and held her aunt's hand.

"I'm heading over to the inn," Andrea informed everyone after breakfast. "Marg called. The furniture I ordered for the lobby and sitting area has arrived. I'm going to help set it up."

"I'm coming too," Aurora informed her mother.

"I'm heading into town with Jamie to pick up a few things for a project we're working on. He should be here soon," Cora chimed in with her own plans.

"Well, I guess that leaves you and me, Mom," Jo threw across the island to her mother. "Want to spend the day with me?" she offered.

Becky's brows raised in surprise before she smiled in appreciation. “I would love to spend time with you, honey. What do you have in mind?”

“I haven’t quite thought it through, but maybe we could take a stroll down to the rose garden Dad built for you, and we can take it from there,” she suggested. “Who knows if there’s time, but we could probably go get an ice cream cone in town afterward.”

“I’d love that,” her mother replied. “Let me help with these dishes, and then I’ll head up to take a shower.”

“That’s fine, Mom. We’ve got it under control,” Cora intercepted. “You can go freshen up.” The other sisters nodded their agreement. Becky had no choice but to head upstairs to take her shower. Aurora left them to make a call to James, her fiancé.

Cora and Andrea began clearing the island of the dirty dishes and taking them over to where Jo was using the detached pipe head to rinse the dishes of any debris before washing them with soap.

“So, about Mom’s party,” Cora started, “I’m heading into town with Jamie to get the rest of the fixtures for the platform he’ll be setting up at the back of the inn.”

The other two bobbed their heads in understanding.

“Drea, did you find the album with Mom’s old photos?” Cora turned to the middle sister to ask.

“We found it. Rory’s helping me with the story for the video. Also, remember I’ll need you two to come by the room to add your appreciation speeches to the film.”

“Okay,” they agreed.

“So, everything looks to be on track for this weekend. Kerry says she’s started prepping to make the birthday cake, and Chef says the preparations are coming together.”

“Oh, I forgot. I promised Daniel I would help with the meal prep,” Jo explained, happy that she could contribute to their mother’s celebration.

“That’s great, Jo,” Cora commended. “I’ve already invited

some of Mom and Dad's closest friends. Uncle Luke and Aunt Stacy are lining up the rest of the family." Cora sighed with satisfaction. "This is going be the greatest celebration of all. A day to remember. It has to be."

All three sister's half smiled, reminded of the urgency of celebrating their mother's birthday on the weekend, cognizant that this could be her last birthday with the family.

Chapter Eight

It was the day before Becky's birthday, and the house was at full capacity. Jules had arrived three days ago. Cora had gone to pick her up at the ferry terminal in Clinton. Jo knew her sister had been itching to confront her daughter about the news she'd sprung on her just over a week ago but had refrained from badgering Jules after she'd expressed that she didn't want to talk about it right now.

Jo and Andrea told her to give Jules space to process the situation and was comfortable enough to talk to her about it. Jo could see that Cora was struggling to remain quiet but was happy that she was trying to respect her daughter's wishes.

Erin, Jules's older sister, would be arriving today but without her boyfriend Brian. Tracy also called to inform her that she and Josh would be arriving later in the afternoon.

Jo had been sitting in the den with the rest of the family when her phone rang.

"Hello?"

"Hi, Jo. It's Kerry," her cousin greeted from the other end of the line.

"Hey, Kerry. What can I do for you?" she asked, perking up. She noted that everyone's gaze had been on her, including her mother's, even though they continued to converse.

Lifting herself from the couch she'd been sitting on, she walked over to the window furthest from her mother and her keen hearing.

"I just wanted you to know that the package is ready for pick up. I'll be here until this afternoon, but I'll leave instructions with my staff to give it to you if you come after," Kerry informed her.

"That's great news. I was actually thinking of heading into town within the hour," Jo told her cousin.

"Okay. Let me give you the address."

After writing down the Heavenly Treats address, Jo said goodbye and hung up with Kerry. She walked back to her seat beside her mother to continue with the conversation.

"I'm heading into town," Jo announced after half an hour had passed. "Do you guys need anything while I'm out?" she asked.

"Can you bring me back some soft pretzels and sauerkraut, please, Aunt Jo?"

At Jules's weird request, Jo noticed Cora's eyes focus on her daughter before looking away and shaking her head.

"Sure, sweetie," Jo replied, giving her niece a genuine smile even though her weird cravings seemed to be confirmation of her situation.

No one else had a request, so Jo slipped out of the house and backed the Rav4 out of its parking space and drove off the property toward her cousin's bakery. It wasn't difficult to find it because even though she hadn't gone out much since returning to the island, she still knew her way around— besides, the street names were still the same, and Kerry's shop was between Midway Blvd and Goldie Road where the intersected I-20.

The moment Jo laid eyes on the bakery, she was in love.

The outside was mostly covered in Boston ivy. The glossy green color of the foliage would soon transition into shades of orange, yellow, and red come fall. The orange-colored honeysuckle blossoms reached down from the roof of the building to join the ivy providing a wonderful contrast of colors. If that weren't enough, the potted crotons and ferns lined the pathway that led to the entrance; even though she couldn't see clearly through the paneled windows, the smell of freshly baked treats wafted to her nose and called out to her sweet tooth.

When she made it inside, she couldn't stop herself from gawking. She felt as if she was in pastry heaven. There was a variety of simple and difficult-to-make treats looking back at her from the glass display at the front of the store.

"Hi, welcome to Heavenly Treats. How may I help you?"

Jo looked up at the woman with light blond hair and striking green eyes, who gave her a friendly smile as she waited on her to order something.

"Hi..." Jo squinted to make out the woman's name tag. "Anne, I'm Josephine. I'm here to see my cousin, Kerry. Is she here?"

"Oh, yes. She said you were coming. She's in the back. Let me get her for you," Anne offered.

"Thank you."

The young woman disappeared through the door behind her. Jo took the time to inspect some more.

"Hey, Jo," Kerry greeted as soon as she stepped through the door. She wore an apron with the baker's logo stitched over the top, and her auburn hair pulled back from her face, a handkerchief tied over the top Jo assumed to keep away stray hairs.

"Hey, Kerry," she returned, smiling in greeting.

Kerry came around the display and drew her into a hug that Jo returned. "The cake's around the back. Come on," she continued to say, leading Jo through the door she had just emerged from.

The room, which turned out to be the kitchen, was decked out with the latest appliances and state-of-the-art equipment. A four-tiered deck oven and a twelve-burner industrial stove stood at the back where the exhaust hood was mounted. A long table stood in the middle of the room, and the large refrigerator stood in one corner. Pots and pans were either on hooks in the walls or spilling out of the overhead cupboards. She noted a loader tray filled with freshly baked muffins, cookies, donuts, and bread. All this caused her mouth to water. She wanted to sink her teeth into each of the fluffy dough to taste the sweetness of the sugar that dusted their surface or lick the jelly from their pockets.

"That's Wyatt, our resident pâtissier." Kerry threw her head to the side to point out the man in a chef jacket by the stove, stirring whatever the contents were in a mixing bowl with a wooden spoon.

At the sound of his name, the man who had otherwise been preoccupied turned his head to look at them, Jo more so than the others, his light amber eyes scrutinizing her.

"Wyatt, this is Jo, my cousin," Kerry introduced.

In response, he lifted his hand and gave a small wave, which Jo returned with a "Hi" of her own.

"So, the cake is her favorite. It's coconut angel cake," Kerry revealed. She walked to the refrigerator to retrieve the cake.

It was a three-tiered masterpiece. White frosting covered the base to the top, with red, pink, and purple rose petals adorning all sides and dusted with coconut flakes.

"This looks so delicious, and I haven't even tasted it. I'm sure Mom is going to be beside herself with joy when she sees it," Jo complimented her cousin's skills.

Kerry beamed. "Thanks, Jo. That's the reaction I was going for." Kerry turned to Jo. "You have to keep it in the walk-in fridge at the restaurant, then take it out approximately two hours before the party so that it can acclimatize and be ready for serving," she instructed Jo.

"Okay, no problem," she agreed. "I'm going to need the recipe for this beautiful cake as well." She gestured to the cake on the counter.

"Sure, I'll text you the recipe," Kerry agreed. "Let me help you get it to the car."

The two women carefully brought the cake out to Andrea's car with no mishaps involved.

"So, I'll see you tomorrow," Jo said in departing.

"Yeah, see you."

Jo pulled off and made her way over to the mall to quickly grab a few things and her niece's weird request before heading back. She brought the car to a stop before the Willberry Eats.

She liked the rustic feel and the unassuming guise of the exterior. She also liked the fact that the large windows on either side of the wooden door were paneled and slightly tinted, giving away nothing of what to expect from the inside. She thought about some upgrades that could be made on the outside to make it even more welcoming and made a mental note to discuss it with her sisters.

Jo marveled again at just how beautiful the interior of the restaurant truly was. Every surface was stained wood, from the walls to the floor to the tables and chairs that were evenly spaced throughout the room. She especially liked the fact that the ceiling was exposed with the rafters of the gambrel roof on full display and supported the high ceiling fans and hanging lights for extra lamination. She thought about possibly commissioning Kerry to supply a few of her heavenly treats to add to the dessert menu, but that was something she would have to take up with the head chef whom she was currently seeking.

"Hi, Mrs. Hamilton-Boyer, would you like a table today," the bubbly waitress who she met just a few days ago greeted with a broad smile.

"Hi, Pat, no, not today. I'm actually here to see Chef Daniel," she replied to the young woman.

"Sure thing, Mrs. Hamilton-Boyer, right this way."

Jo followed the young woman to the back, where she could see and hear Daniel instructing a young man to add more pepper to whatever was cooking on the stove. She waited for him to finish before making her presence known.

"Well, hello, Jo. It's a pleasure to see you this afternoon," he greeted, bringing the back of her hand to his lips to lightly brush it with a kiss.

Jo couldn't help the warmth that spread over her whenever he greeted her in such a manner. She was still unaccustomed to this. It didn't make her uncomfortable, though, just slightly surprised each time.

"What brings you here today?"

"Well, I have Mom's cake for tomorrow in the van. I was wondering if you could help me to get it to the refrigerator," she requested.

"Of course," he agreed. After leaving instructions with the line chef, he followed her out to her vehicle and assisted her in lifting out the cake box and taking it back inside to place in the walk-in fridge.

"About tomorrow's menu," she started as soon as the fridge door had been secured.

"Yes. What about it?" he asked, hands clasped behind his back while he waited for her to continue.

"There's something that I wanted to add to it. I know it's a lot, but I really want to do this for her. I thought about not doing it because it was something she and Dad had at their wedding, and I didn't want to make her cry, but now I think about it, I think it's a good way for her to still feel close to him like he's there cheering her on," she explained.

"Jo, you don't have to explain your reason. It's okay, I get it," Daniel informed her. "Just make sure you're here early to help me prepare all of this. Everything has already been prepped. Give me the list of ingredients for the new recipe, and I'll get them later," he instructed her.

She gave him a grateful smile before rattling off the items needed for the special dish. "So, I'll be here bright and early to help you," she informed Daniel, who had walked her back to her car.

"All right, see you then," he replied, pushing away from her car as she started the engine.

Within three minutes, she pulled up to the house, noting that Josh's Ford pickup was parked alongside the others. A huge grin made its way onto her lips as she went inside to greet her daughter.

She met no one on the inside, but she could hear laughter coming from outside. Pushing open the back door and walking onto the porch, she made her way down the three short steps that led to the patio, where she could see her family laughing and chatting away while the smell of burgers and hot dogs being grilled drifted to her nose.

She could see Andrea, her mother, Erin, Jules, Aurora, Tracy, and Josh all seated in a semi-circle in the bamboo chairs. Jamie and Cora stood by the grill talking while Jamie flipped the meat.

"Mom, you're here." Tracy rushed to her mother, who pulled her in for a hug, grateful for her presence.

"Hi, honey. How was your ride down?"

"It was okay," Tracy replied.

"I'm glad you made it."

"Me too," Tracy replied. A small, uncertain smile graced her lips.

Jo wondered what that was about but didn't get time to address it.

"Hi, Aunt Jo," Erin greeted, giving her a big hug. Josh came and hugged her, and shortly after, everyone settled down once more, and the conversation continued to flow as the family joked and reminisced on old, treasured memories.

Soon, the family moved the gathering to the porch. Becky sat on the swing with Jules and Tracy sitting on either side of her. The others sat in the armchairs and the bamboo chairs.

"Mom, I was thinking that since the girls will all be here for your birthday tomorrow, we should make reservations to have dinner at the inn," Cora suggested to her mother. "Something small and intimate."

"That sounds wonderful, sweetie. I love that idea. I'm happy that I'll be getting to celebrate this day with all of you after all these years," Becky beamed at her daughters and granddaughters, who all sat around her.

"We're happy to be here for this, too, Mom," Jo murmured, reaching for her mother's hand and squeezing it affectionately. Soon the conversation changed as the family got back to their light bantering and laughter.

Jo brought the wineglass to her lips and sipped as she looked around at her family, either holding a bottle of beer or a glass of wine in their hands, enjoying their time together. Her eyes glistened with unshed tears, a smile on her lips.

"What a beautiful sight, right?" Cora asked from her side.

Jo looked over at her sister and nodded her agreement. "I just wish Dad was here to see it all."

Chapter Nine

"Okay, everyone, we have approximately four hours to transform this place into something magical. Let's get to work, people," Cora issued from the newly built deck at the back of the inn. Jamie had finished putting it together just last night, and now with its height, it overlooked the water perfectly. This was where their mother would be sitting as the highlight of the party took place. Aqua and pink silken curtains adorned the backboard just behind it.

Andrea had taken Becky shopping to get her hair and nails done to keep her occupied and away so she wouldn't figure things out. In her mind, the highlight of today would be the reservation for dinner at the inn. Jo couldn't wait to see the look of surprise that was bound to cross her face. She couldn't wait.

Jo helped Cora hang the birthday banner on the backboard while the girls blew up the purple, white, and gold balloons to be used to finish adorning the deck and the rest of the space. Jamie had commissioned his men to set up the tables and chairs and any other heavy-duty lifting.

Jo looked over at her daughter, who was sporting a frown

and looking out across the water with her arms folded across her chest. Something was definitely wrong.

"Hey, honey." She bumped her daughter's shoulder with hers in greeting.

Tracy looked over at her mother and quickly plastered on a smile that didn't quite reach her eyes. "Hey, Mom," she greeted her back. "What's up?"

Jo turned to her daughter and reached out to run her fingers through her sandy brown hair. She searched her light brown, almost amber eyes, trying to figure out if something was wrong with her? "Are you all right?" she finally asked.

"Yeah, Mom... I'm fine. I'm just a little tired," Tracy answered.

Jo couldn't help the nagging feeling that there was something her daughter was keeping from her. "Are you sure?"

"Mom, I said I'm fine. Can you give it a rest?"

Jo reared back slightly, surprised by her daughter's forceful tone and words.

Tracy's eyes widened in surprise before they shuttered. "I'm sorry, Mom. I didn't mean to talk to you like that," she apologized.

"It's okay, honey. You said you were fine, and I still pushed. I'm sorry," Jo responded, soothing her hand down her daughter's arm. "I just want you to know that you can talk to me about anything," she reminded her daughter.

"I know. Thanks, Mom." Tracy gave her mother a small smile.

Jo left her daughter feeling torn. There was obviously something she wasn't telling her, but she wouldn't push her. She would wait on her to come to her. That didn't mean she couldn't talk to the one person that possibly knew what was going on with her, though.

"Hey, Josh. Can I have a minute?"

Josh's hazel eyes shifted from where he was unpacking chairs up to his mother-in-law.

"Sure thing, Mrs. B," he answered, straightening up to walk over to her.

Jo looked back to see her daughter was preoccupied, talking to her cousins.

"It's about Tracy," she spoke as quietly as she could.

"What about her?" Josh asked, perplexed.

"I don't know. She seems a bit off, and I can't help but wonder if something is the matter." Jo looked at Josh seriously. "As a mother, I am asking you, is my daughter all right?"

"She's fine," Josh reassured Jo.

She still couldn't shake the feeling that something was wrong, but for now, she would have to let it go. She made her way over to the restaurant to see how things were going and to help Daniel finish the preparations.

"Hey," she greeted the man as soon as she entered the kitchen.

"Hey," he returned with a smile.

"Everything on schedule?" she asked, reaching for an apron to tie over her clothes.

"Yes, everything is going as planned," Daniel answered.

"Great. Tell me what you need me to do," she offered.

"Okay. I need you to make the tartar sauce for the fish and shrimp, and after that, I need you to sauté the mushrooms and onions and make a vinaigrette dressing for the pasta salad," he instructed.

"Sir, yes, sir." Jo saluted Daniel, provoking a laugh from him.

"All right, get to work, Private," he said with the most serious face he could muster.

Jo laughed at how ridiculous he looked, trying to keep in his own laughter while trying to maintain his composure. As if triggered by her own laughter, he chuckled, shaking his head.

"All right, we really need to get to work now," he spoke through his chuckles.

The two worked in sync, getting everything ready. When she was finished, she excused herself to go freshen up.

When she made it back over to the inn, the guests had already started to arrive. Jo hadn't seen their cars because Cora had instructed everyone to park over by the house as the plan was that Andrea would take their mother straight to the inn when they arrived.

"Hi, Uncle Luke, Aunt Maria. You're both looking very lovely," Jo complimented her uncle and his wife.

"Thanks, JoJo. You're looking quite lovely yourself," Uncle Luke returned.

"Absolutely stunning," Aunt Maria joined in.

Just then, Cora came running through the back door of the inn. "All right, everyone in position. Andrea says they're five minutes away," she alerted the guests.

Jo waited in anticipation for her mother to come around the side of the building to be pleasantly surprised. Andrea would tell her that she needed to go pick up something from the gazebo behind the inn and have Becky follow her.

"They're here. Get ready," Cora whispered.

Just then, they heard Andrea's voice loud enough to alert them of their presence. Three seconds later, the two women rounded the side of the building.

"Surprise!"

Becky jumped in surprise, holding her chest. Her wide brown eyes began to register what was before her, and as realization kicked in, a wide smile came to her lips as tears of joy glistened in her eyes.

"Happy birthday, Mom," Andrea, who was closest to her, said, pulling her into a loving embrace.

When she released her, Cora went up to hug her mother, followed by Jo.

"I can't believe you all came here to celebrate my birthday. It truly means a lot to me," Becky spoke with her hand across her heart.

"You deserve to be celebrated, Becky." Aunt Stacy slowly drove up in her mobility scooter and stopped before Becky. "You are an extraordinary woman, and we all know that Sam would want you to continue celebrating your birthday even though he's not here."

Becky reached down and grasped the older woman's hand. "Thank you, Stacy. I truly appreciate it."

After everyone had greeted and congratulated Becky on another milestone, the partygoers made their way inside the lobby of the inn, where the food had been set up buffet style. Everyone took their plates and stacked as much food as they could handle before taking their seat at the tables outside.

Jo made her mother's plate and brought it to her. When her mother looked at the content of her plate, her eyes widened in surprise before she raised them to her daughter, questioning.

"Truffle mushroom pasta," she confirmed. "I remember you and Dad had said that was the best dish from your wedding. I thought I would recreate it for you as that was one of the happiest days of your life, and it started with this meal," she explained.

Becky's eyes watered as she reached up to curve her palm over her daughter's cheek. "Thank you, sweetie. This is... I love you very much, my flower," her mother finished.

Jo gave her a sweet smile before reaching down to kiss her on the side of her head.

After everyone had gotten their plates, family members and friends alike got up to make a toast to Becky.

"I have worked for Becky for over ten years now, and in that time, she's been more than just my employer— she became my friend and, dare I say, even my family. Becky, you are a gem that, with time, has grown even more beautiful, and I see no one that deserves such a day of appreciation as you do. To Becky." Marg raised her glass to the woman who sat looking down at the people that had come to celebrate her, tears glistening in her eyes.

"Thank you," she mouthed to Marg. Jo gave her a subtle nod of approval for her sweet toast.

After that, Uncle Luke got up to make a toast of his own. "Becky, it always amazed me how my brother managed to hit the jackpot when he got to marry you. You have been a wonderful addition to this family, showing us the meaning of unconditional love as you remained unwavering in your love for Sam and for your girls and this family. You are a sister to me and Stacy, and I want you to know that we love you very much. Seeing your girls back here and ready to support you on the rest of your journey makes me a happy man."

Everyone raised their glasses after the toast before taking a sip of their beverage.

"All right, everyone. If you could just turn your attention to the screen on your right. Cora, Jo, and I have made a video for our mom that we would like you all to see," Andrea announced to the guests before making her way over to the projector screen that was set up.

The screen lit up with the words "Happy Birthday to you, Mom." The screen flashed to still photos of their mother, showing a photo of her at one year old, then at five, then seven. The progression continued when their mother went on her first date with their father, and then it skipped to a snippet of their wedding video. The video then progressed through the birth of each daughter and moved on to the birth of her grandchildren. At the end of the video was Cora, Andrea, and Jo talking about their mother.

"My first inspiration to follow my dreams came from my mother. She had reminded me that I could be anything I chose to be because I was smart, and I had a lot to offer. Mom, I know

I may have never said this to you before, but I am who I am today because you are the first person that believed in me, and for that, I am grateful. I love you."

Jo felt herself tearing up at Cora's message to her mother and looking over at the deck where her mother was dabbing her eyes, she could tell that she was deeply affected by it as well.

Andrea spoke about how her mother represented the hope she thought she had lost all those years ago but now only realized that it had always been there because she had always known that her mother's love was still available even when she was running.

Then it was Jo's time to speak. She tensed as she waited for her face to appear on the screen.

"Hi, Mom. I just want you to know that I love you very much, and I appreciate everything that you did for me during my grief. Even though I tried to push you away with everyone, you never gave up on me. You kept reaching out and reminding me that you were there for me and that you loved me. Even though I didn't admit it then, I want you to know that I thought about your love for me every day, and from that time, whenever I started to spiral, I would remember that you still loved me. I love you, Mom."

Jo chanced looking over at her mother to see the tears now fully running down her cheeks without hindrance. She placed her hand over her heart as she stared at her daughter, a reminder that she was always in her heart. Jo returned the gesture.

Chapter Ten

After the cake was brought out and the guest sang happy birthday to Becky, she opened a few of her presents, thanking everyone. She then spent some time catching up with her old friends.

"Jo," Ben, her cousin, called out to her.

"Hey, Ben. I'm glad you were able to make it," Jo greeted, accepting his hug.

"I'm happy too. What you guys did for Aunt Becky was truly special," he commended.

"We felt it was the right thing to do," she replied.

Just then, she saw Marg waving at her. Jo raised her hand and waved her over.

"Hey, Marg, what's up?" she asked as soon as the woman was in hearing range.

"I apologize for interrupting, but Chef Daniel has been looking for you," she informed Jo.

"Oh, okay. Ben, we'll catch up at another time, I promise."

"No problem," Ben assured her.

"Oh, shoot my manners." She lightly slapped her forehead,

turning from Ben to Marg. "Marg, I'm not sure if you've met my cousin Ben, Aunt Stacy's son. Ben, this is Marg. She works at the inn," she introduced. "I gotta go." With that, she jetted off, leaving the two to get acquainted.

Three hours later, the party was winding down. Only Uncle Luke, Aunt Maria, and Aunt Stacy remained. They were by the gazebo sitting and reminiscing on the good old days. The three girls used the time to start cleaning up the party items. Jamie and his workers had already started disassembling the platform and packing up the tables and chairs and other heavy equipment.

"I think Mom's tired now. Maybe I should take her home so she can rest," Andrea spoke as they took a break to watch their mother. It was the same concern that had been swirling in Jo's head for the past half hour. Becky had stifled a few yawns even while trying to keep up with the conversations, but it was obvious that she was beat.

"I think that's a good idea," Cora, who stood on the other side of Jo, agreed.

"Yeah. I agree," Jo gave her input.

At this, Andrea made her way over to the gazebo to speak to their mother about turning in. Five minutes later, the older folk walked over with Andrea.

"We're gonna get a move on now, girls," Uncle Luke gave out as soon as he was standing before them. "I didn't realize it was so late, and we need to get Stacy back to the house," he explained.

"That's okay, Uncle Luke. We're glad everyone was able to make it," Cora said, allowing Luke to wrap her up in his arms.

He did the same to Andrea and Jo.

"What you girls did for Becky today... it was truly wonderful. I'm proud of you girls."

At this, Jo broke out into a grin as the warmness of his words encouraged her.

As soon as they left, Becky turned to her daughters with a bright smile. "Thanks for today, my beautiful daughters. This was one of the best days of my life," she confessed, reaching out to give each of them a long hug and kiss on their cheeks.

"We're happy we've made it special for you, Mom. You deserve it," Jo replied, placing a soft kiss against her mother's temple. Becky squeezed her hand.

"Where are the girls?" Becky asked, looking around.

"Oh, they're inside the inn packing up," Cora informed her.

"Okay. Are you sure you girls don't need a hand finishing up here?" she asked.

"No, Mom," Cora refused. "You're tired, we can tell, and besides, today was your day to kick back and relax."

"All right. Well, I guess I'll see you all later," she said, smiling tenderly at Jo and Cora.

After packing the gifts Becky had received from the party into the Jeep, Andrea drove her mother up to the house to prepare for bed.

Jo and Cora returned to what they were doing.

"Hey."

Jo looked up to see Jamie's gaze trained on her sister, a gentle upturn to his lips.

Cora straightened up, returning the smile. "Hey," she replied softly.

Jo looked back and forth between the two as a grin broke out on her lips at the sweet display before her.

"I'm leaving now, but I was wondering if there's anything else you'd like me to help you with," he advised.

"Oh, no. We're almost done here," she returned.

"Okay," Jamie replied, scratching the back of his head as he looked from her to Jo.

Sensing that he probably wanted to have a private conversation with her sister, Jo decided to give them space.

"I'm going to see if they left anything by the gazebo. I'll be back in a few," she informed Cora. "Thanks for your help today, Jamie." She smiled at the very tall man whom she suspected she would soon be calling her brother-in-law.

"It was my pleasure, Josephine. I'm glad I could make Mrs. Hamilton's day special."

Jo gave the man another warm smile before turning and heading for the gazebo.

From her vantage point, Jo could make out the two holding hands and Cora throwing her head back in laughter at whatever Jamie said to her. After a few more exchanges, Cora's hands went around Jamie's waist as his hands came over her shoulders. He planted a quick kiss against her hair before releasing her and walking away. Cora turned to watch him.

At the display before her, Jo's face lit up with the excitement she felt for her sister. From what she had seen and known of Jamie, she could tell that he was the best thing that could have happened to her sister at this time. He looked at her and treated her as if she mattered to him more than anything else. Jo remembered how that felt; even with all she knew now, she was sure of one thing, her husband had loved her greatly.

"Jamie can't seem to get enough of you," she spoke to her sister as soon as she was back at her side. "I can tell he really cares about you."

Cora turned and gave her sister a knowing smile. "I know he does, and I care about him too, but..."

At her hesitation, Jo cocked her head, interested in the excuse her sister was about to make.

Cora sighed. "I just don't want to move too quickly," she reasoned.

Jo reached over to run her palm over her sister's arm in a soothing fashion. "You don't have to rush anything, Cora. He seems like a real patient guy who will wait until you're ready to fully share yourself with him. Just don't let fear stop you from accepting your second chance at love."

Cora squeezed Jo's hand in gratitude. "Thanks, JoJo, it means a lot coming from you." The sisters hugged, taking strength in the warmth generated from the gesture.

"I know we still have a lot to work through, but I'm happy that we got this time to do it and be here for Mom. She needs this, us getting along, being here," Cora explained as soon as the two separated.

At her sister's statement, Jo's mind flashed back to the day in the kitchen with her mother.

"Cora, there's something I didn't tell you..."

Cora arched her brows in concern, waiting.

"It's about Mom. I made coffee for her about two weeks ago, and the cup fell out of her hand and shattered, then her words were slightly slurred." Jo took in a gulp of air before releasing it with a heavy sigh. She finally turned her gaze to her sister, who stared back at her in alarm. "I've never seen her like that, Cora. You should have seen the look of fear and shame in her eyes; it broke my heart, and worse, I didn't really know what to do." Jo looked up at her sister, her eyes reflecting the weight of her next words. "I'm scared, Cora. After losing so much, I-I- don't know how I'll cope with losing her too." Jo brought her hands around her torso to hug herself tightly. Voicing the turmoil she'd been feeling over her mother's illness to her sister made it all the more real, and it felt as if something inside had started to crumble.

"I'm sorry you had to witness that, Jo." Cora released a sigh before pulling her sister against her once more.

Automatically Jo's hands circled her sister's waist as she drew comfort from her. Slowly the tears ran down her cheeks to drip down her chin unto her chest. "I've got you, too, Jo," Cora soothed. "I'm here for you. I want you to know that you can always talk to me when it gets too much to bear."

Jo nodded against her sister's chest, grateful for the offer. "Thanks, Cora."

"You're welcome, sweetie," her sister replied as they separated. "There's something that I need to tell you too," Cora admitted, her eyes reflecting the sadness she felt. "Mom had an episode on the third night I was here."

"What..." Jo replied incredulously.

"We were having dinner at the restaurant, and she had a muscle spasm. She couldn't hold the fork in her hand, and we had to end the night." Cora detailed the incident.

"Oh my God," Jo responded as her hands went up to cover her mouth.

Cora gave her a rueful look. "We knew it was coming, Jo, but we just have to be there for her more than we've been doing."

Jo nodded in answer. "Just tell me what you need me to do," she implored her sister.

Soon the two settled back into packing up the rest of the decorations. "Cora," Jo called out to her sister, halting her movements.

She hesitated before asking, "Have you noticed anything about Tracy?"

Cora looked back at her in confusion. "No. Like what?" she asked, straightening up.

Jo sighed as she too straightened up. "I'm not sure," she said slowly. "She just seems a little off, like something is bothering her and... I don't know. I guess I'm worried about her," she confessed.

"Jo, Tracy is fine," her sister assured her. "Maybe you're reading a little too much into her actions because of all that has happened in the past year and how it has affected her. You're probably projecting," Cora reasoned.

Jo opened her mouth to speak but then closed it when no words left her lips.

"Jo, she's fine," Cora affirmed.

"You're right," she agreed. "I'm probably just overreacting."

She still couldn't shake the feeling that there was more than what met the eyes. Her interactions with her daughter felt different, as if she was keeping something from her. Suddenly her mind flashed to the revelation she had gotten a few months ago that had shattered her even more than the death of her husband. It was something she wasn't sure she would ever be able to share with anyone. She was too ashamed by it to even dwell on it too much, and if her daughter found out what she knew, she knew the level of devastation it would wreak on her. She prayed to God she would never find out about it— at least not until she thought Tracy was strong enough to handle the truth.

Chapter Eleven

"Hello, welcome to the Willberry Inn. How can I help you?" Jo smiled at the young couple standing before her with equally bright smiles of their own.

"Hi, we made reservations to stay here for a week," the woman spoke, coming closer to the reception desk with the man following close behind. "It's under the names Selena and Mark Johnson," she clarified further.

"Okay. Let me check on that for you," Jo replied. Turning her focus to the computer screen, she pulled up the Google booking calendar. "Ah yes, your reservation is here," she confirmed, turning to smile at the couple once more. "The room is already prepared for you. I'll take you up as soon as you sign here." Jo pushed the signature book and a pen over to the couple. The man took the pen to sign.

"Great. Now let me show you your room." Jo grinned, moving from around the desk. The couple followed her toward the grand staircase that led to the first and second floors. From over her shoulder, she could see the couple running their hand along with the smooth mahogany wood of the banister in appreciation.

"Is this your first time on the island?" she asked as they stepped onto the landing of the first floor.

"Oh, yes, it is," the bubbly female replied while nodding profusely. "Mark and I just got married. We wanted to do something outside the box, you know, get away from the city and all its hustle and bustle. So naturally, we wanted it to be somewhere where we would be able to enjoy nature and just more time spent with each other," she divulged.

"Oh, that's lovely," Jo spoke, turning toward them. "You've come to the right place then. There is so much that Whidbey has to offer. I know you won't be disappointed you came," she said confidently.

Both guests smiled warmly at her.

"I really like the beauty of this inn," the woman stated. "The minute I saw it on the website, I just knew that this is where we should honeymoon, and then when I got here and saw it up close and just how beautiful the grounds were, I knew we had made the right choice. Right, honey?"

"Yes, right, darling," Mark readily agreed.

Jo chuckled at this, knowing that Mark's answer had been to appease his wife's excitement. She could tell that Selena was talkative by nature as opposed to her husband, who she could clearly determine that he was shy and reserved. But he looked at his wife and hung on to her every word. Jo was certain he told her that he truly adored her and quite possibly only made the trip for her sake

"I'm glad you like it," Josephine replied. "This inn has been in my family for five generations, but before that, it was a colonial home belonging to the once governor of Whidbey. We haven't done much in terms of renovations because we wanted it to maintain that authentic feel of the past and the history behind its existence. At the same time, adding a few modern touches gives it the perfect balance, so it doesn't feel overly antiquated," she explained.

"Well, I'm glad you didn't change much because I am totally in love with this place," Selena expressed.

"Be sure to say that in your reviews," Jo spoke half-jokingly, earning a laugh from both guests. "Your rooms are this way." She gestured toward the corridor closer to the set of stairs on the east side of the double grand staircase.

The couple followed her dutifully until she came to a stop at the door to their room. She unlocked the doors with the set of keys for the room, then pushed it open and ushered the couple inside. She could tell that they were pleased with what they saw and that, in turn, satisfied her.

The room, like all the others, could be described as a small self-contained studio space. The queen-sized bed stood against the far wall opposite the door. An antique wooden wardrobe filled out the space between the bed and the wall adjacent to it. A small sitting area adorned by a corner sofa and a small coffee table was on the next side of the bed and turned toward the large French doors that led out to a private balcony overlooking the property and the waters. Just to the left of the entrance to the room was the en-suite bathroom, separated by a door. The only thing missing was a small kitchenette. Most meals were prepared by the restaurant, or they could use the kitchen on the ground floor.

"Oh, wow, this is truly magical," Selena gushed. She made her way over to the bed to run her hand over the duvet on the bed before heading toward the French doors and opening them. Jo chuckled at the loud gasp that traveled to her ears as the woman stood out on the balcony, enjoying the view. "Honey, you have to come to look at this. It's spectacular," she urged her husband.

Placing the suitcase at the foot of the bed, her husband stepped out on the balcony to join her.

Jo was very happy that they liked the room. She hadn't encountered one guest that had a complaint against the inn, and she was glad— the more positive reviews the inn got, the more appealing and noticeable it became to potential guests.

After advising the couple of the restaurant's hours and suggesting a few site attractions, they could visit while on the island, Jo returned to her reception post. A few hours later, Marg walked in.

"Hi, Josephine," she greeted warmly.

"Hi, Marg," she replied, the woman's warm, bubbly personality instantly triggering a smiling response to hers. "You're early. Your shift doesn't start until six, and now it's just..." Jo looked down at the watch on her wrist before lifting her gaze back to the woman before her. "It's only four-fifteen."

"I'm sorry, Jo, I just couldn't stay home," Marg responded apologetically.

Jo realized that even though the woman before her was smiling and her voice remained light and friendly that something seemed to be bothering her. She could see her dark brown eyes seemed duller than she'd ever seen them behind her black-framed glasses.

"Marg, is everything okay?" she asked in concern.

Marg's eyes widened in surprise before shuttering. She opened her mouth several times as if to say something but closed it each time, resembling a fish gasping for air. Jo noticed the slight shake of her head before she looked back at her with a small smile that didn't reach her eyes.

"It's fine, Jo," she assured her. "I'm just a bit worn out. My grandmother is sick and has me worried," she confessed, wringing her hands before her.

"Oh, no. I'm so sorry, Marg," Jo consoled the woman who had become a dear friend to her and her sisters in such a short span of time. "Is there anything we can do?" she asked, coming around the reception desk to rest her hand on the woman's upper arm.

Marg grasped the hand on her arm and squeezed Jo's fingers in gratefulness. "Thank you for the offer, Jo, but no," she declined. "My grandmother is getting the best care she can, but it's not enough. She hasn't been responding to the treatments, and the doctors don't know what to do."

Jo's heart broke for Marg. She understood the feeling of helplessness. She watched as the woman sat on one of the sofas and released a heavy sigh.

"I just need to be here, Josephine. I need to take my mind off everything," she expressed.

"I understand," Jo replied, taking the seat opposite her. "I just wish there was more I could do to help."

Marg reached over to take her hand in hers. "You're understanding and offering to help is enough," she said sincerely.

The two sat and chatted until Jo's time was finished. She left Marg to finish out the day and headed for home.

Ten minutes later, Jo was at the house. Laughter coming from the back caught her attention, and so she decided to detour there. She found her mother, Jules, Tracy, Aurora, and Erin sitting on the back porch. The girls were all engrossed in whatever Becky was telling them, and no one saw her approaching. She took the time to observe her daughter laughing along with her nieces, the usual tenses she had felt since she arrived on the island were gone, and her face lit up, reminding Jo of her happy-go-lucky daughter, who was able to smile in the midst of adversity.

Becky was the first to acknowledge her approach. "Hi, sweetie. How was your time at the inn?" she asked as Jo ascended the three steps.

"Hi, Mom, it was good. A couple checked in this afternoon, and I helped them get settled," she informed her mother before placing a kiss against her temple.

Straightening up, she looked over the girls who had smiles, except for her daughter, whose lips were set in a thin straight line, her eyes wary. Catching her mother's eyes, she quickly looked away. Jo felt her heart constrict with fear.

"How are you girls doing?" she asked, forcing a smile.

"We're good, Aunt Jo," Erin replied. "Grandma was just telling us stories about you and Mom and Aunt Drea," she further explained.

"All good things, I hope." She turned to her mother with a knowing smile, appreciative of the fact that her mother was filling in the girls on their history as a means of drawing them closer.

"All good, I promise," Becky replied.

From the corner of her eye, she could feel her daughter's stare.

"Where are Cora and Drea?" she asked.

"They're inside preparing dinner."

"Okay, let me pop in really quick and see if they need any help," she said before making her way through the back door.

She found Cora removing a tray of baked chicken from the oven. Andrea stood by the kitchen sink cleaning and chopping vegetables.

"Seems like you guys have everything under control," she spoke, making her presence known.

"Hey, how was your day at the inn?" Cora greeted.

"It was fine," she replied simply. "Need any help?"

"Not really," Andrea answered this time. "Everything's almost done. We're just about to set the table, plus you must be tired."

"I'm okay," Jo replied. "I'll just head back outside and make sure Mom doesn't tell the girls anything embarrassing about us." She slid off the stool and made her way toward the back door. She halted in surprise to see her daughter by the door.

"Hey, sweetie, are you all right?" she asked, approaching her cautiously.

"Can we talk? In private," her daughter requested.

"Oh... sure," she agreed even as her heart rate accelerated. "Let's go for a walk," she offered, leading her daughter back through the door.

After letting her mother and nieces know that she was going for a walk with Tracy, the two made their way down to the sunken patio and took the pathway that led toward the dock. Jo rubbed her sweaty palms against the fabric of her jeans, her nerves getting the better of her the closer they got to the dock. When they finally made it, she went to the end of the dock and sat on one of the Adirondack chairs. Her daughter followed suit and sat in the chair opposite hers.

As the two continued to sit in silence, looking out at the water, Jo took the time to admire the pinkish-orange hue of the sky heralded by the sun slowly disappearing below the horizon while the water shimmered from the last burst of brightness.

"Mom, I need to ask you something, and I really need you to be honest with me," Tracy finally spoke, breaking the silence between them.

Jo schooled her face to remain stoic even as her heartbeat tripled its normal rate.

"What did Dad do?"

Her eyes widened as the façade slipped at her daughter's directness. "Wh-what do you mean?" she asked, flabbergasted. "Why are you asking me this?"

Tracy stared at her mother, her eyes contemplative. After a minute of just staring and Jo feeling trapped by her daughter's unwavering stare, Tracy spoke again. "A man approached me back in Arlington the day before we arrived here. He was saying some things that just didn't make sense, and I didn't want to believe him, but the more I think about it, the more my gut is telling me that it's true," she said, her eyes filled with sadness.

"What did he tell you?" Jo managed to get out as her fingernails dug into her palms from how tightly she fisted her hands.

Tracy turned glistening eyes toward her mother. "He said that Dad's accident didn't happen the way it was reported. He said I should ask you because you knew what actually happened, but if you refuse to tell me, he'll do it himself."

At her daughter's revelation, Jo's heart slammed against her chest, and her lungs seemed to empty themselves of all the air as the walls of her throat tightened, making it difficult to breathe.

She knew then that this could be a life-altering moment between her and her daughter. She prayed that things would be all right.

Chapter Twelve

"Mom, it's okay. You can tell me anything. It's just you and me."

Jo couldn't bring herself to look at her daughter. Her eyes glistened with the unshed tears as she continued to stare out at the water. The lump in her throat prevented any words from escaping her lips. She had dreaded this moment as soon as she found out over a year ago. Now, here she was sitting with the one person she was trying to protect from the truth. It turned out all her efforts had been in vain.

"Mom. Please. Talk to me." Her daughter's soft voice and hand, now resting on top of her clasped ones, caused the dam to break, allowing her tears to flow freely down her cheeks.

Finally, she turned to lock eyes with her daughter, who looked concerned and anxious. "I never wanted you to find out like this, sweetie," she murmured, regret lacing her voice.

Tracy didn't reply. Her brown eyes stared back at her mother, waiting for her to continue.

Jo took in a gulp of air before continuing. "The man that

approached you, his name is Jared Hindle. He was your father's boss and a partner at the firm." Jo paused, trying to put her words together. Finding no other way to say it, she sighed resignedly before turning back to her daughter once more.

"Charles, at the time of his death, owed the firm half a million dollars for an unauthorized investment he made using one of his clients as the primary funder. The investment tanked, and he lost the money. He had to be working double-time to try and recover the lost funds, and he was under a lot of stress. I now realize that's what led him to the bottle— to start drinking."

Jo exhaled, remembering the first time she had discovered the smell of strong liquor on his work shirt. She hadn't confronted him then, but the next time she had, his excuse was that he usually had one glass with his meal during the long days at work to relieve some of the stress. She hadn't fully bought the story but had decided to let it go. Maybe if she had been more direct, she wouldn't be having this conversation with Tracy, and Charles and Nick would still be alive.

"I found out a week after the accident that it wasn't, in fact, an animal that ran into the road and caused Charles to lose control of the vehicle, but rather that he was driving under the influence. The toxicology report revealed that the alcohol level in his blood was higher than normal," she finished while looking out at the horizon again.

When she turned to look at her daughter, she noticed the tears steadily rolling down her cheek as her mouth opened and closed, the shock of her mother's confession rendering her speechless.

"I'm so sorry for not telling you, honey. I just wanted to protect you from all of this...I...I didn't want you to blame your father for Nick's death or for your memories of him to be tainted by this." Jo gently reached over to touch her daughter, but Tracy pulled her arm away as if she'd been burned before standing to her feet, facing her mother.

Jo recoiled from the scorching glare fixed on her daughter's face, and she gasped audibly. She'd never seen her daughter look this angry and directed at her.

"Oh, my Go—" a guttural sound left Tracy's throat as she was unable to finish her statement.

Jo's heart shattered at the sight of her daughter. "Trac—"

"How could you keep this from me? Who gave you that right?" her daughter threw at her accusingly.

Jo flinched again from the venom in her daughter's tone. Salty tears blurred her vision as her heart burned with the regret she felt for hurting her.

"Tracy, I'm so—"

Before she could finish her apology, Tracy turned away from her and ran toward the path.

"Tracy! Tracy, wait!"

Her daughter didn't stop. She continued running until Jo was no longer able to make her out behind the wall of trees blocking her line of sight. She collapsed in the chair as sobs racked her body.

* * *

"Jo, what's going on? Tracy is back at the house crying and packing her bags, saying she and Josh are leaving the island."

Jo heard the franticness in her sister's voice, but she couldn't bring herself to look at her. She was just too numb with the pain and the weight of what she'd done. She continued to stare across the horizon, the sun had long set, but it was still bright enough to see the reflection of the pink overhead clouds in the water.

"Jo, you're crying," her sister spoke softly as she leaned by the chair. Cora reached up to wipe away a few drops of her tears that refused to stop falling. "What happened, Sis? Talk to me, please," Cora pleaded.

"Charles was under the influence of alcohol the night of the accident. He wasn't swerving to avoid a wild animal. He lost control of the vehicle because he was drunk," she informed her sister bitterly.

"Oh no. I'm so sorry, Jo," Cora said sympathetically.

Jo released a dry laugh. "That isn't even half of it. Do you want to know what my loving husband, who I held in such high esteem as a man of integrity, did, hmm?" she asked. "He invested one of his client's retirement funds in a venture that he thought would work. Long story short, it didn't, which left him with a debt of half a million to repay. You would think as his wife that he would have confided this to me, and we could have tried to work it out together, but no, he chose to turn to the bottle to work out his stress, and now his boss is harassing me to give back the money they had to reimburse the client or risk him making it public knowledge of what Charles did and what caused the accident." After that mouthful, Jo felt drained. "Now, my daughter hates me because she can't see that I only did this to protect her and what we have left," she sniffled.

Cora pulled her sister from the chair and engulfed her in her arms. Jo clung to Cora as if her life depended on it as she released all the pain, the regrets, and remorse she had been holding in for so long.

"How could he do this, Cora? How could he do this to our family?" she cried.

"Shh. It's okay. It's going to be okay, Josephine," Cora consoled, holding her head against her chest. But Cora's words did nothing to alleviate the sinking feeling she had in the pit of her stomach.

Cora moved to sit in the chair and brought her sister against her. She didn't mind the weight. It reminded her of when they were younger and how she used to console her youngest sister by taking her onto her lap and running her hand over her hair as she comforted her.

Jo was too drained to move, so she welcomed the warmness of her sister's embrace. The two remained in that position for a long time until the sound of footfalls against the boardwalk of the dock caused Cora to turn her head to see who it was. Jo was too tired to look.

"What's going on?" she heard Andrea ask from above her. "Tracy is crying and won't tell us what happened, and now Jo."

"Tracy found out some news that was... unexpected," Cora replied hesitantly.

"How so?" Andrea asked.

Cora went on to relay everything Jo had told her.

"Oh my god, that's terrible," Andrea gasped in shock.

Jo felt a pair of hands wrap around her from behind as a set of lips were placed against her temple.

"I'm so sorry this happened to you guys, Jo. I can't imagine how hard it must have been to hold on to such information for so long with no one to talk to. I should have been there more for you, but I promise I'm here now," her sister murmured against her ear.

She was still far spent and could barely open her mouth to reply. "Thanks, Drea," she mustered as much strength as she could to say.

"I'm going back to the house to see if I can get Tracy to change her mind and stay so this can be sorted out," Andrea told them, straightening up.

"That sounds good," Cora agreed.

After a long time of them sitting arm in arm, Josephine finally disentangled herself from her sister and sat on the other chair.

"So, what exactly did this ex-boss of Charles say he has on him?" Cora asked.

Jo sighed. "Nothing more than what I told you. He wants

me to pay him over the five hundred thousand dollars from the insurance money and from the house sale. I ignored his messages and blocked his number. I guess that's why he sought out Tracy, to force my hand, I guess."

Cora nodded as she listened to her sister speak. "Are you sure he's telling the truth?" she finally asked.

"He showed me the evidence that Charles invested the money and that it failed," Jo answered.

Cora gave her a skeptical look.

"I know that it could be a forged document, but that's not all… I remember Charles on the phone about a month before the accident. He was talking to his boss, promising that he would get it back before it was noticed missing. I didn't think much of it but now thinking about it and the fact that he had been drinking more than he ever had in all his lifetime, I'm inclined to believe Jared."

"Okay," Cora returned simply, nodding as she mulled over her sister's words. You don't owe this Jared fellow anything, Jo," she finally said.

Jo looked over at her sister in confusion.

"What I mean is, the only thing he had over you was the fear of Tracy finding out about the accident and the money, but that has already been taken care of, so what can he do? It's not like he can make the information public. If he did, it would open up the firm to closer scrutiny. Take it from me; my years as a journalist has taught me that big firms and corporations like to settle things of this nature outside the courtroom and out of the public domain because there is always the fear of ruin from things of this nature," Cora explained.

"True, you may have a point," Jo replied, her tone of voice questioning.

"What I'm saying is that Jared can't force you to turn over the insurance policy to him. It's your money that was left to take care of you and Tracy. Any debt that Charles had died with him that night. Don't let Jared intimidate you. Drea and I got you. You don't have to go through this alone anymore, Sis."

Relief rolled over Josephine at her sister's words. Getting up, she went over to embrace Cora, who had also risen from her chair to receive the hug.

"Thanks, Sis," she said simply.

"Anytime, Jo. And don't worry about Tracy. She'll come around. She just needs time."

At the mention of her daughter, Jo's slightly hopeful mood dampened once more. She wanted to believe those words, but all she saw were her daughter's angry brown eyes staring back at her.

Chapter Thirteen

The ping of her phone woke Jo from a fitful sleep. Reaching over to the bedside table, she grabbed her phone and opened it. It was a text message from her daughter. Josephine quickly sat up in the bed and opened it.

Hi, Mom. Josh and I are back in Tacoma... I need some time to think, so please don't call me. I love you, but I can't talk to you right now. I'll call you.

A tear slipped down Jo's cheek as she hurriedly typed out a message to send her daughter. She had called Tracy's phone nonstop last night to apologize and make sure she'd made it home safely, but she hadn't answered. When her calls started going straight to voicemail, she called Josh, but he hadn't answered either. She spent most of the night up, worrying about them— worried that something could have happened to them, but knowing that it was probably just her paranoia.

Ok, sweetie. I understand. I want you to know that I am so sorry, and I didn't do this to hurt you. I thought I was protecting you. When you're ready to talk, I'm here. I love you.

A sob slipped through her lips as the phone slipped

through her fingers unto the bed. As the tears trickled down her face, her heart became increasingly heavier at the thought that she had possibly lost her daughter's trust forever and that the relationship would never be the same. She couldn't handle the implications of it all, and she slid down the bed and rolled onto her belly to bury her face in her pillow as the tears flowed.

An hour later, when the bright sun rays streamed through her slightly shifted curtains, Jo pushed herself out of bed and took a much-needed hot shower. As she looked in the mirror above the sink in her bathroom, she could only describe herself as looking like death. There were dark circles under her eyes, and her skin looked sallow. Sighing heavily, she took off her nightgown and stepped under the warm pelting sprays in the shower.

As soon as she made it back into her room, she heard her phone ping. She hurriedly moved to it, hoping that it was her daughter, and her face fell when she realized that it was Chef Daniel. Still feeling dejected, she chose to leave the message until she had finished dressing.

Jo made her way downstairs and was immediately drawn by the voices and the aroma coming from the kitchen. Aurora, Jules, Erin, and her boyfriend Brian sat around the kitchen island eating and talking while Cora stood by the cabinets sipping what Jo presumed was coffee.

"Good morning, everyone," she greeted as lightly as she could.

Cora's gaze instantly shifted to her with concern in their gray-blue depths before she masked it with a smile.

"Good morning, Aunt Jo," her nieces greeted in unison.

"Good morning, Jo. How are you feeling?" Cora asked, standing up straighter.

"Beat," Jo answered truthfully before adding, "And hungry."

"Great. Let me put together a plate for you." Her sister smiled with relief.

Jo pulled up a chair and sat at the end of the island as she waited for her sister to plate out some food for her. She was famished. She had skipped dinner last night and had instead opted to drink a quarter of a bottle of merlot in her room as she cried and tried to call her daughter. It hadn't been enough to impair her senses, but it had made her nauseous, and this morning she was queasy and hungry.

As soon as Cora placed a plate filled with scrambled eggs, sausages, hash browns, and toast before her, Jo couldn't help but gush at the presentation. She quickly dug into the food, enjoying the creaminess of the eggs massaging her taste buds and causing her mouth to salivate.

"Where's Drea?" she asked between bites.

"Oh, she went by the inn to fill in for Marg because she had an emergency."

"Okay," Jo replied in understanding. Her mind flashed to what Marg had told her about her grandmother yesterday. She hoped everything was okay.

"So, what are you guys up to today?" she asked the girls and Brian.

"Oh, we're actually leaving today, Aunt Jo," Erin spoke up.

"Already?" Jo asked, surprised.

"Yeah, Brian and I both have to get back to our jobs," Erin further explained.

"I'm visiting James's parents this week, so I have to leave too," Aurora added.

"Okay. I guess I just thought we had more time to do some fun stuff together."

"I'll be here, Aunt Jo. We can do some fun stuff," Jules jumped in.

"That's great, Jules. I would love that," Jo answered truthfully. From her vantage point, she could see Cora staring intently at her younger daughter. She realized that they probably hadn't spoken about Jules's revelation.

"Good morning, everyone."

Jo turned to see her mother waltzing into the room with a bright smile and shining eyes as she placed a kiss on each of her granddaughters' cheeks. She even gave Brian a peck.

"You're in a chipper mood," Cora surmised as she offered her mother a cup of coffee and started dishing out her breakfast.

"I am," Becky confirmed. "I feel like I have a new lease on life. All of my girls are here." She turned smiling eyes on them for emphasis.

"Why did Tracy leave in such a hurry last night, though? I thought she was planning to stay for the weekend." Becky turned questioning eyes toward Jo.

Jo quickly averted her eyes, afraid her mother would see the pain reflected there.

"Tracy had to leave because she had some registration issues she had to clear up with her university," Cora jumped in, saving her sister from having to explain the situation.

Jo looked up at her sister and gave her a grateful smile.

"Oh, I hope it all works out then," Becky returned with concern.

"I forgot. Chef Daniel asked me to be his sous chef until Malia comes back from maternity leave," Jo announced to the group, hoping to shift the questions away from her daughter.

"That's great, Jo," Cora exclaimed excitedly. "I know it's not as big as the bistro you worked at back in Tacoma, but at least it is up your alley and will keep you occupied."

"Yes, for sure," she replied simply as the others congratulated her.

Josephine quickly escaped the kitchen as soon as she was finished eating as she didn't want to witness the happiness her family was exhibiting just being around each other— not when her own daughter didn't even want to talk to her. Sighing, she opened the front door and made her way toward the walkway that led to the inn and the bistro.

She was hardly able to appreciate the scenery around her as her mind kept going back to her daughter's angry look. She wished she had a machine that could take her back in time so she could fix all the mistakes she'd made.

As the inn came into view, she decided to pop in to see how Andrea was doing before continuing on her journey to the bistro.

"Jo." Andrea seemed surprised to see her. "What are you doing here? Is everything okay?"

Jo gave her a slight shake of her head as her lips quivered. Andrea hurriedly rounded the reception desk and engulfed her in a hug as she crumbled.

"I miss them, Drea," she sobbed against her sister's chest.

"Why did they have to die? How could Charles have been so selfish?"

A guttural cry escaped from Jo once more. She leaned into Andrea's embrace as the anger and the pain slowly subsided.

"He did this...h-h-he...my daughter hates me because of something that he did. Now my whole family is gone."

"Oh, honey, that's not true," Andrea finally spoke up. "Tracy is angry now, but she'll come around," Andrea cooed, running her hand over her sister's hair. "Look at me," she implored, lifting her sister's head to look into her teary eyes. "Tracy will forgive you, Jo. You want to know how I know she will?"

Jo shook her head in response, unable to use her words.

"Because Aurora forgave me for hiding the truth about her father from her for her entire life, and our relationship has never been stronger," Andrea explained, trying to get her sister to see reason. "Tracy will realize that you only did what you did to protect her. She'll come around. Trust me."

Again, Jo nodded in acceptance of what her sister had just told her.

"I want you to know that it's okay to feel how you feel about what happened to Charles and Nick. I do believe that man loved you with his whole heart. Sometimes we make mistakes and trying to spare our loved ones the disappointment we feel they will have because of our messing up will sometimes only make the situation worse. He made a mistake, Jo, but never doubt that he loved you and the kids very much."

"I know he did, Drea," Jo finally got her voice to cooperate. "It just hurts that he didn't tell me what was going on, and now I'm left to deal with the repercussions of his actions." She sighed.

Andrea placed her arm over her sister's shoulder, hugging her to her side. "We'll get through it all together, Jo. You, me, and Cora," she promised.

Jo left the inn feeling much better than she'd felt since getting up. She was greeted by Pat and Suzie, two of the three servers that worked at the Bistro. After informing them that she would be filling in for Malia as sous chef, they took her to the kitchen, where Daniel was already preparing for the lunch hour.

"I see that I am just in time," she commented.

Daniel turned to look at her, relief showing in his gray eyes as a bright smile blessed his lips. "You're here," he greeted.

"In the flesh." She laughed. She hadn't replied to his message, so she could see how he assumed she would not take up the offer. "So, what do you need me to do, Chef?" she asked, buttoning up the chef coat she'd taken with her and then securing the toque blanche over her already swept-up hair.

"So, what was the deciding factor in you accepting my offer?" Daniel asked after a good fifteen minutes of them working side by side to stay on time for the lunch hour.

"The promise of free food at the end of my shift," Jo joked.

At this, Daniel let out a deep chuckle, and Jo joined in.

"You will have to come up with a better answer than that, Jo," he replied.

Daniel saw Jo hesitate. Jo watched as his eyes narrowed slightly as he stared at her without blinking. *Can he see or rather feel that something is off with me?*

"What about the opportunity of cooking with one of the best chefs I've ever met?" she finally asked, trying to divert the situation.

Daniel glanced around the kitchen as if looking for something. "Where is he?" he asked, looking perplexed.

Jo laughed at this. "So, you really want me to spell it out, do you?" she asked.

"I'm waiting." Daniel smiled broadly, revealing even, white teeth.

"I'm not saying it because it seems I've already inflated your ego a little too much." She smirked, turning back to the fish she had been filleting.

When he didn't immediately respond, Jo turned her head to the side to look up at him. She was surprised to see the intensity of his steel-gray eyes fixed on her.

"You know, if you ever want to talk about what's bothering you, along with being called one of the best chefs, I have also been called one of the best listeners," he offered.

Jo widened her eyes in surprise at his statement before they shuttered, and she turned her attention back to the fish. "I'm fine," she spoke in a dismissive tone. Realizing how it must have come off, she lifted her head to the man once more and gave him a small grin. "I'm fine, really."

After a few agonizing seconds, Daniel gave her a dazzling smile. "Okay," he accepted. "Let's get this meal together before the hungry mob gets here and cuts off our heads for making them wait too long."

Jo laughed at his silliness.

Chapter Fourteen

"Carrot, cat, Colombia, Cauliflower."

"It's not a flower. It's a vegetable." Jo laughed at the man walking beside her.

"Says who?" Daniel challenged.

Jo looked at him incredulously. "Umm... the whole world."

"Oh, yeah? Well, that's still my final answer, and since it has the word flower in it, then it is a flower," he stated, as a matter of fact.

Jo stopped to shake her head at the man walking before her, a huge smile on her face as a result of his goofiness.

"What?" He turned to her innocently.

"You are such a cheat." She meant to come off more serious but couldn't dampen the broad smile on her lips.

Daniel grinned at her. "At least it got you to smile," he concluded triumphantly.

"That it did," she agreed, shaking her head and taking the few steps to catch up to him.

The two had stayed back after the dinner hour to clean up the dirty dishes as Pat left because of an emergency, and Daniel didn't want to leave the task to Suzie alone. Afterward, he'd offered to walk Jo home. Even though she had planned to use the time it took to get to the house to mull over all that had happened in the past forty-eight hours, she'd surprised herself by agreeing. Now here they were playing a game he had suggested.

"We're at D now," Daniel said, reminding her it was her turn.

"Okay. Let's see. Dragon fruit, dog, Denmark, daisies," she replied confidently.

"Are you sure you're not just making that one up?" Daniel asked, looking over at her.

She couldn't see his eyes clearly as the walkway lights didn't provide that amount of illumination, but she could almost tell that they were glinting from mischief.

"Oh, get out of here. I know you must have heard of dragon fruit," she replied, lightly tapping his shoulder.

Daniel chuckled. "Of course. I was just interested to see how you would defend your answer."

"Well, we're at E now," she spoke, reminding him that it was his turn.

Daniel chuckled once more, which caused her to look up at him questioningly.

"It seems we'll have to pick this game up tomorrow," he explained, jutting his chin toward the house.

She hadn't realized that they had arrived by the back porch. Turning to him, she gave him a grateful smile. "Thank you for making sure I made it home in one piece, Chef Daniel." She curtsied.

At this, Daniel let out a deep chuckle. "It was my pleasure, my fair maiden, Josephine." He bowed deeply, eliciting a giggle from Jo. Straightening up, he continued, "See you tomorrow."

"Good night."

Daniel left, retracing his steps, and Jo watched until he was out of sight. She turned and made her way up the steps and made her way to the door. Raised voices coming from the family room left of the back door were the first thing that greeted her when she stepped inside. Confused as to what the commotion was about, she walked into the room in question.

"How could you be so irresponsible, Jules? You're not even finished with school. How could you have let this happen?" she heard her sister's raised voice berating her daughter.

Just as her niece began speaking, Jo walked in to see her and her mother at opposite ends of the room.

"Well, thank God you have Erin, the responsible one, right?" Jules exploded. "At least you can finally admit it. I'm the screwup, but don't worry about it because I'm sure perfect Erin will make up for all that."

"Don't put words in my mouth, young lady!" Cora screeched. "The fact is you were irresponsible. You had your whole life ahead of you, and this is what you chose to do...mess up your future."

Jules looked at her mother with incredulity before her eyes narrowed into tiny, angry slits. Jo decided to step in.

"All right, you two need to stop before you say something you'll both regret," she interjected, stepping in the middle of the two.

"Jo, this doesn't concern you. She needs to know that she's made the biggest mistake of her life," Cora threw over her.

Jo whirled around to face her sister. "Cora, stop," she pleaded, but that only seemed to fuel her sister's anger.

"You know what, Jo? Worry about your own issues with your daughter. Like I said before, this doesn't concern you."

Jo reared back at the hurtful comment as she widened her eyes in surprise, unable to comprehend what her sister had just said, but then as if her brain caught up with the implications of her insults, Jo's eyes registered the hurt she felt.

Cora's eyes widened in realization. "Jo—"

"All right, that's enough," Becky ordered, entering the room with a scowl. "Cora, how could you speak to your sister in such a manner? I raised you girls better than this," she chided. "I will not tolerate this kind of behavior in my home," she finished, staring pointedly at her oldest daughter.

"Josephine, what I said was out of line. I'm sorry," Cora apologized, but Jo couldn't look at her. The hurt was still palpable to her.

"I'll make it up to you. I promise. Jules, can you come with me so we can finish talking. I promise it's just to talk."

"Okay," Jules agreed.

Jo didn't realize that she hadn't moved from where she stood until her mother placed a gentle hand on her shoulder. "Let's sit, sweetie," she offered, moving toward the couch.

Jo followed her mother on legs that felt like rubber, and when she made it to the couch, she collapsed on it.

"Are you okay?" Becky asked, her voice laced with concern. "You can talk to me, Jo," she implored when her daughter still hadn't opened her mouth to speak. Reaching over, she drew her daughter by her shoulder closer to her.

"I... I don't know where to start," Jo admitted tiredly.

"You can start by telling me exactly what Charles got himself in," her mother said.

At this, Jo whipped her head around to look at her mother with surprise.

"I may not always offer my advice because I want you girls to give me a chance to be there for you without feeling like I'm pushing you, but I normally know more than I let on and what I know is that the accident wasn't an accident," Becky revealed.

At this, Jo broke down, allowing the tears that seemed to be ever at hand since last evening to flow down her cheeks. Becky gave her daughter a sympathetic look before drawing her head down to rest in her lap.

"Everything will be okay, sweetie. Just let it all out and

let me be there for you. Let me help you," she cooed, smoothing down Jo's hair before wiping a few of her fallen tears.

Jo sniffled. "Charles got himself in trouble for losing a client's retirement fund on an unauthorized investment," she explained. "He started drinking because he couldn't get back the money and, on the night... on the..." she couldn't finish her statement.

"He was drinking before the accident," Becky stated rather than asked.

Jo could only nod to confirm the spoken words were true. After a full five minutes of building up the strength to continue to confide in her mother, she began again. "The firm had to repay the client. After that, I received Charles' life insurance policy on a technicality because they had waited over seventy-two hours to test the sample instead of the forty-eight hours that was the standard time. One of the partners and his boss at the firm reached out to me to tell me what he had done. I was devastated by the fact that he had been under the influence, and now I was learning that he had committed a white-collar crime."

Becky continued to soothe her daughter, creating a calming environment for her to feel comfortable telling her everything.

"I didn't want to tell Tracy because I didn't want her to think of her father differently than the man she'd known him to be, and I certainly didn't want her to blame him for Nick's death... In the end, she still found out, and now she's angry at me for keeping this from her, and I don't blame her." Jo sighed, defeated.

"Josephine, you did what you thought was best for your daughter. You can't keep beating yourself up for that," Becky encouraged her daughter. "Tracy will come around. She just needs time to work through her emotions toward the whole situation, but she'll come around." Becky kissed her daughter's temple as she comforted her. "As for the other situation, it will work itself out. Don't worry about it."

Jo reached up and gave her mother's hand a grateful squeeze. "Thanks, Mom."

"Anytime, sweetie," Becky replied.

"Did I ever tell you about the trip your father and I went on to France in 1970? That was before any of your girls were born."

Jo turned her face up to look at her mother. "No, you didn't," she answered, intrigued.

"Well, it was the best and the worst trip of our lives." She chuckled lightly as her mind seemed to travel to the time in question.

"What happened?" Jo asked.

"Sam got robbed unbeknownst to us. We went to this restaurant to have a lovely meal, and at the end, his wallet was missing. We kept promising the owner that we would come back to pay the bill, but he wouldn't have it." Becky laughed at the memory.

"What happened then," Jo asked, fully invested.

"He took us to the kitchen, gave us aprons, and ordered us to scrub the big pots and pans to pay off our meal debt."

"Oh, now that must have been awful and humiliating," Jo surmised.

Becky smiled softly. "At first, it was, but then by some bizarre twist, we started enjoying it. From there, we applied for jobs in the same restaurant, and that summer, we spent days sightseeing and at nights washing pots and pans." Her eyes glazed over as nostalgia set in. "What I wouldn't give to have a day like that with him again."

Jo gave her mother a sympathetic look.

"We never had a vacation like that again." Becky smiled wryly. "When we came home, he spent time trying to grow the business, and so, little trips like those became infrequent."

Jo reached over and touched her mother's arm gently. Becky took her daughter's hand and grasped it comfortingly. From there, the stories about her and Sam became more entertaining with fewer sad moments, and the two women retired to their rooms at peace.

Chapter Fifteen

Jo stared unseeingly at the roof in her room. The blackout curtains were pulled back, leaving the sheer ones over the glass windows, which allowed the darkness from outside to seep into the already darkened room. The stillness in the air was palpable and only seemed to magnify her racing thoughts.

Her mind kept replaying the way Cora had used her problem with Tracy to hurt her in the heat of the moment. She'd thought they were making progress in their already fragile relationship, but maybe she had jumped the gun a little early. Maybe they had just been kidding themselves into thinking that they could go back to the way they were—twenty-five years was probably too much time to make up for. Perhaps, coming back to Oak Harbor itself was a mistake. Her stomach clenched at the thought.

Jo stayed in the same position until the first signs of light from the hidden sun dispersed, illuminating the dark skies. She took it as her cue to go for a run to clear her mind.

Scooting to the edge of the bed, she swung her legs over

before standing and stretched out the tightness she felt in her shoulders and lower back.

After washing up, she donned her running gear and headed downstairs. The house was still as quiet as it had been since the moment she opened her eyes over two hours ago. As far as she could tell, everyone was still asleep, but she didn't mind.

When her sneaker-clad feet touched the gravel of the walkway that led from the porch to the arched driveway, Jo took off running.

She breathed in and out as she went, her chest moving up and down as her lungs worked hard to balance the exchange of gases in her body. She had been running for the past hour, overextending herself. Her calves prickled with signs of fatigue, but she didn't want to stop, not until she had made it to the end of the narrow beach trail that bordered Flintstone Park.

The run had been to clear her mind and regroup, but her thoughts continued to race ahead of her feet. She felt frustrated, but still, she willed her body forward. Running along the shoreline, taking the salty air into her lungs as the cold morning air whipped her face, usually helped her get her mind back to harmony, but today her thoughts chose to run renegade against her desires.

She finally slowed her steps as she felt her legs tightening and threatening to give way. She stopped completely and leaned over, grasping her thighs as she took quick breaths to replenish the oxygen in her lungs.

Spotting a boulder a few feet from where she was, she straightened up and made her way over to rest against it. Jo rested her lower back against the smooth rock face, and her feet parted for balance as she stared out across the horizon. She could see cormorants moving about on the water's wavy surface before they disappeared into the depths on their quest for fish. She potted a bald eagle gliding a few feet above the water, barely a flap from its magnificent wingspan. These were the things that made her love the outdoors so much— the opportunity to experience and appreciate nature in its purest form.

Just then, her phone pinged. Reaching into the pocket of her leggings, she pulled out the device and held it up to see a message from Tracy. Her heart rate quickened as she went to open it and read.

"I'm really sorry, Mom."

Jo released the breath she hadn't realized she was holding. The message gave her hope— her daughter was ready to talk to her. Pressing the call button, she put the phone to her ear and waited anxiously for her daughter to pick up. After the third ring, Tracy answered.

"Mom, hi," came her daughter's soft, unsure voice.

"Hi, sweetie...I got your text," she answered equally as soft. She held the phone tightly to her ear, waiting for her daughter's response after a long pause.

"I'm really sorry, Mom," she finally replied.

Tracy's pained voice coming through the speaker tugged at Jo's heart.

"Oh, sweetie. You don't have anything to apologize for. The fault was all mine," she tried to appease her daughter.

"But Mom, I-I-... I shouted at you. I-I—"

"Tracy, sweetie, don't. You had a right to react the way you did. I kept something very important from you, and that's something I will regret for a very long time." Jo wished her daughter could see how much she regretted her actions, but her words would have to suffice.

"But that's the thing, Mom... none of this was your fault," her daughter interjected. "I wish you had told me, and I didn't have to find out the way I did, but I know, even while I was angry at you, that you only did it to protect me." Jo could hear Tracy draw in a long breath, then release it slowly. "I can't imagine how devastated you were to find out that Dad was an embezzler and that he caused Nick's death. How... how could he have done that to our family, Mom?"

Jo felt her heart break from the raw pain in her daughter's voice. It was the same pain she'd felt. Those were the same words she'd asked herself many lonely nights as she cried into her pillow, waiting for sleep to take her tired body. She wished she was right there by her side to give her a hug, to run her hand through her hair, to kiss her temple, and tell her that it was all going to be okay.

"Sweetie," she started cautiously. "What your father did was wrong on so many levels, and we're suffering because of it, but I need you to know that even though he did all that, he loved you and your brother very much. He would have done anything to keep you both sheltered and happy. He made mistakes, but I choose to believe that he was still a good man. I know it will take you some time to get there, believe me, I know, but I want you to find it in your heart to forgive your father and focus on the good parts— everything you knew before this."

The silence from the other end of the line told her that Tracy was struggling with what she'd just said. "Sweetie, no matter what, he was your father," she coaxed.

"I don't know if I'll ever be able to move past the fact that Nick is dead because of Dad's carelessness, Mom," her daughter said, deadly calm.

Jo opened her mouth to speak but quickly closed it. What could she say to her daughter to make her see that holding on to the anger and feeling of betrayal wasn't healthy? How could she encourage her, knowing it took months for her to get to a place where she could forgive Charles? "I know it's hard, sweetie, and I understand it will take time to get there, but please try to forgive him for me."

At this, Tracy released a frustrated sigh. "Can we talk about something else now?" she asked, changing the subject.

Jo's lips turned down in sadness at her daughter's avoidance. "Okay, sweetie," she softly agreed. "How is Josh doing?"

"Josh is great. He's been very understanding," her daughter replied, her voice less pained. "He helped me realize that I needed to speak to you, that I shouldn't blame you for trying to protect me and deal with this all by yourself."

A smile graced Jo's lips as she listened to her daughter talk about her fiancé with such love and admiration. She knew how much Josh loved her daughter and was happy that the two had each other to lean on. "Josh is a wonderful young man," she praised.

"Yeah, he is," Tracy agreed.

Jo could hear the smile in her voice as she spoke, which caused the corners of her mouth to quirk up. "I love you, Tracy," she said passionately to the speaker.

"I love you too, Mom," her daughter returned.

Jo's heart swelled with joy. "The thought of anything hurting you breaks my heart, but just know that I would never do anything intentionally to hurt you. You are my world. I don't know what I would do if anything happened to you..." she couldn't finish the statement, her mind blocking out the possibility of her daughter ever getting hurt.

"Mom, nothing's going to happen. You have me always," Tracy soothed her mother.

"All right," Jo resolved. "I want to know you're okay at all times, so please call me as often as you can, and I'll do the same," she implored.

"I promise. I will."

A couple of minutes later, the two hung up, and a permanent smile that wasn't there before her daughter called was now etched on her face. Knowing that her daughter forgave her and that they were back to how their relationship always was, gave her a boost of courage to dial the number of the man that had been blackmailing her. She wanted to let him know what she thought about his threats.

"It's about time you came to your senses," came the smug voice of Jared Hindle the second he answered.

Like him, Jo skipped the formalities and got straight into why she called. "How could you make such a move to approach my daughter like that, Jared?" she questioned furiously.

"It was a necessary means to an end," the man replied insouciantly. "It got you to take this seriously and realize that you need to give back the money, didn't it?"

Jo laughed. "You know I was actually considering handing over the insurance money to you, but now, tough luck trying to get it because I am not willingly giving you one red cent," she informed him.

"You're making a big mistake, Josephine," Jared warned. "If you choose to take this road, I will be forced to—"

"To what?" Jo interrupted, "tell my daughter? Well, surprise! She already knows, and we've become stronger because of it. So, I will repeat myself... You. Are. Not. Getting. A. Dime." She hung up, not waiting for his response. Feeling a sense of accomplishment, she pushed away from the rock and turned toward the path that would take her back home.

When Jo finally entered the house, she was sweaty and tired. It didn't seem as though anyone was downstairs, but just as she made it to the steps, she heard talking coming from the family room.

"That is not a word."

"It is so, Grandma."

Jo found her mother and niece seated before a partially populated Scrabble board on the coffee table. They were partially turned away from her and were too engrossed in the game to notice her presence.

"Dudevorce?" she heard her mother ask skeptically while giving Jules a pointed look.

"Yes, Grandma," the young woman laughed. "It's one of the newly added words."

Becky pulled down the spectacles she had perched on top of her head until they covered her eyes. She took the iPad her granddaughter held out to her.

"Hmm." The woman scrunched her face, narrowing her eyes at what she read. She looked from the iPad to Jules and then back at it as if reluctant to accept the fact that the word actually existed.

Jo smiled at their interaction. She was happy that her mother was getting the time to interact with her grandchildren in a way she had not been able to for so long.

"It seems everything is being turned into sensible words nowadays," Becky spoke begrudgingly, earning a chuckle from Jules.

Jo stifled her laugh as she watched her mother being a sore loser. Just then, she felt a tap on her shoulder. Turning around, she came in contact with her sister's blue-gray eyes that stared at her apprehensively.

"Hey," Cora greeted simply.

"Hey," Jo responded. Her lips were slightly upturned.

"Umm...can we talk?" Cora asked sheepishly.

"Yeah, sure," Jo agreed.

Jo followed Cora to the back door and stepped onto the porch after her. The two stood by the railing, looking out at the trees on the horizon blocking the water from this side of the house.

"I'm really sorry for what I said to you yesterday, Jo. It was out of line and selfish."

Jo turned her head to see her sister already looking at her, remorse clouding her features.

Jo reached over and took her sister's hand in hers and squeezed it as she turned her face in the direction it was previously. "It's okay," she assured Cora. "We all say things in the heat of the moment."

"I shouldn't have said what I did in the heat of the moment or not," Cora shot.

Jo could tell that her sister truly regretted what she'd said, and she appreciated her efforts to accept her actions and not make excuses for them.

"Cora, we'll have misunderstandings, and we'll have disagreements, but at the end of the day, we're sisters. I really don't want us to go back to the way things were before Dad's death," she reasoned.

Cora gave her a smile of gratitude, but the glint in her eyes told Jo she wanted to say more on the matter.

"Tracy called," she added quickly.

Cora's eyes widened in surprise and interest. "Oh, yeah? What did she say?"

At this, a wide grin broke out on Jo's face. "Well, she's forgiven me for not telling her, and I guess you can say we're back to normal," she beamed.

"Wow, that's wonderful, Josephine. I'm happy that you guys are back to where you once were. Now, the two of you can start processing all these emotions together."

Jo smiled. "What about you and Jules?" she asked before she could stop herself.

At the mention of Jules, Jo noticed Cora's smile slipped a bit.

Chapter Sixteen

"Another order for the special. Top sirloin medium-well with baked potatoes and pan-seared salmon with the lemon herb rice and a serving of pickled asparagus. Hold the sauce."

Jo groaned as she reached for the order sheet to go over everything that Suzie, one of the servers, had just rattled off to her. She looked over to Daniel by the stove, looking back at her with a smirk as he held the tongs ready to turn the lamb shanks browning in the skillet for the previous order. "You wanted to know what a real dinner crowd looks like here. Well, you got it," he said, still smirking.

Jo rolled her eyes at him. "I'm quitting," she pouted. Daniel laughed at her look of petulance before turning back to the fire. Jo turned her attention to the young woman awaiting instructions. "Take these to table four, and this order will be ready in the next fifteen minutes."

Suzie nodded, taking the small basket of sliced bread and the jug of cold water. Before she exited through the double stainless-steel doors that led to the main hall, she looked back at Jo with a warm smile. "Welcome to the family."

Jo returned her smile before turning toward the chaotic yet orderly kitchen. An abundance of ingredients, mainly seasonings and vegetables, lay on one of the prep tables, while another table held chopping boards, knives, and bowls for wet ingredients. She and Daniel had been on their feet with no break for the past two hours, and by the looks of it, they would be on their feet for another two to finish the orders and clean the kitchen. The crowd that had shown up for dinner this evening had surprised her. It was as if the restaurant was operating a revolving door, as it seemed that the more people left after their meals, twice as many would show up. She wasn't complaining. Josephine was used to this sort of thing back at her old job in Tacoma, but she was surprised that such a small eatery could draw such a large crowd. She hadn't come prepared with the mindset to have so much to do. If the restaurant was doing so well considering its size, perhaps they could afford to expand it and possibly hire more staff. This was something she'd have to discuss with her sisters, though.

"Penny for your thoughts?"

She looked over her shoulder to see Daniel staring at her curiously.

"I was just thinking of how I can get you to fire me," she deadpanned.

"Sorry, that is not an option." Daniel grinned; his steel-gray eyes twinkled with mischief.

"Oh, really?" Jo challenged, turning fully to him with her hands folded over her chest.

"Yup. Not even if you pulled out your toenails and served them as hors d'oeuvres."

Jo made a face. "That's disgusting." She shuddered.

Daniel laughed. "Well, at least you know how desperately I need you here," he said lightly.

Jo felt the heat rising up her neck. Quickly, she averted her gaze and turned back to the table to continue what she was doing before the telltale signs of her flushed skin could give away the fact that she was affected by his words.

"Well, don't get too comfortable. The minute your sous chef is back, I'm out of here," she gestured, pointing toward the door.

She didn't know if he was about to respond because just then, Pat, their next server, pushed her head through the door, her chirpy voice interrupting whatever vibe had been running in the kitchen.

"Is order twenty ready?" she asked.

"Yes. Give me a minute to just plate and garnish this," she heard Daniel respond to the young lady. At this, Pat stepped into the kitchen and waited for the order with her tray in hand.

Jo continued with what she was doing, lightly seasoning the steak and salmon and preparing the frying pans with a small amount of oil.

"Need help?" Daniel sidled up to her the minute Pat left.

"Yes, thanks," she accepted. "Can you prepare the steak, medium well done, while I do the salmon, please?"

"Sure thing," he agreed.

The two chefs worked in unison as if they had been doing this for years, and everything they suggested or added to the dishes complemented the flavors well.

"Taste this," Jo stretched her hand up as Daniel bent his head down to taste the sauce on the wooden spoon she held. She looked up, waiting for his reaction as he rolled the sauce around in his mouth.

"Mm-hmm. This tastes great," he complimented, causing Jo's lips to turn up in satisfaction. "Let me suggest that you add just another teaspoon of oregano and see how that comes out."

"Okay," she readily agreed. It amazed her how eagerly she wanted to please this man, yet back in her old job, when the head chef had shot down her ideas and instructed her to add more ingredients or cut back on something, she'd more often than not, done so unwillingly. Yet, with Daniel, it was different. She seemed to thrive off his compliments and trusted herself more to try new things like the garlic pesto sauce she'd just made. She also liked the fact that he welcomed her suggestions and didn't hesitate to follow her instructions.

"What are you thinking?" Daniel asked her as she kept staring at him.

"How much I like you more than my previous boss." She widened her eyes in surprise at the words that had just slipped out of her mouth. She quickly went into damage control mode. "I mean, you're nicer than my old boss. I appreciate that and the fact that you welcome my suggestions."

Daniel smiled tenderly down at her. His gaze seemed to bore into her soul, seeing more than what was on display. Jo felt her heart rate quicken.

"Is order twenty-one ready?" Suzie asked from over at the door, causing the two to jump back from each other, breaking whatever invisible bond was between them just now.

"Oh, yeah," Jo managed to find her voice.

"Great," the server cheered, unaware of the tension in the room.

Jo plated the salmon with the rice and asparagus while Daniel plated the steak and potatoes.

A frown marred her face as her thoughts went to everything she'd just spewed from her mouth. She hoped her babbling hadn't given him the wrong idea, and she wanted to clear up what she'd said further but was too embarrassed to bring it up. She looked over at the man who was busy preparing the ingredients for the chocolate mousse for dessert. She made a step in his direction when the kitchen door swung open again.

"Jo, there's a lady out there who says she'd like to speak with you. She says she is a friend of your mother."

Jo furrowed her eyebrows as she looked at the blond-haired waitress with bright blue eyes and an effervescent smile.

"Did she give you a name?" she asked Suzie.

"No, she didn't."

Jo excused herself and followed the waitress to a table at the far corner of the room closest to the entrance. The woman sat alone, her gray hair in a neat chignon bun at her nape. Her light brown eyes raised at Jo's approach and a smile of recognition graced her lips. The woman looked familiar, but she couldn't place her.

"Well, look at you, little Miss Josephine, all grown up," the woman drawled. Her accent was distinct and indicated she was from the south, Texas, maybe. Just then, it clicked, and instant glimpses of her past came rushing back.

"Aunt Greta," Jo greeted warmly. "It's so good to see you." She hugged the woman tightly against her chest.

"It's good to see you too, darling," the woman echoed. "Why, I haven't seen you since you turned sixteen years old," she continued to say. "Still, you haven't changed that much that my old eyes can't pick you out of any crowd."

Jo smiled at the petite woman. She was much older now, with loose skin around her eyes, neck, and hands, but she was just as sassy as she remembered her.

"Have you seen, Mom?" she asked the woman.

"Oh no, not yet. I was thinking about taking a room by the inn, and then in the morning, I'll surprise her."

"That's a great idea, Aunt Greta. I know she'll be so happy when she sees you."

After a few more minutes of chitchat, Jo excused herself and made her way to the kitchen.

"Hey, everything okay?" Daniel asked the minute she stepped into the room.

"Oh yes. I just met one of my mom's friends that we haven't seen in years," she informed him.

"That's great," he returned.

"Yeah, I can't wait for Mom to see her. She's going to be so happy."

Daniel smiled at her enthusiasm. Jo averted her gaze. "So, now that we're done for the night, shall we get started cleaning up?" she asked.

"Yes, we should," Daniel answered simply.

The two worked in silence for the next half hour, washing the dishes brought in by the servers before Daniel advised them that they could leave for the evening.

She felt his gaze on her every time he turned his head in her direction, which made her hyperaware of his presence beside her, filling up her thoughts about what he was thinking.

"What is it?" she finally asked, turning to him.

Daniel turned off the faucet and turned to her, eyes unreadable. Jo furrowed her brows, wondering what he was thinking.

"You did well today. I'm proud of you for accepting this challenge," he informed her seriously.

Jo felt a flutter in her chest, and the corners of her mouth curved upward.

"I think you are the best sous chef I've ever worked with, and I don't say that lightly," he continued to say.

This time Jo couldn't help the wide grin that was plastered on her face. "Thank you," she spoke softly, unable to utter anything else.

Daniel smiled down at her tenderly, his gaze boring into her as they had done earlier. Jo felt her heartbeat quicken. She wanted to tear her gaze away, but something was stopping her as if an invisible magnet was keeping them connected.

"We make a good team," he stated, his voice low and raspy. Daniel looked past her eyes, and she wondered what he was looking at. Just then, his eyes lowered to look into hers as he lowered his head. Instantly, Jo panicked. She knew what he was about to do, and yet, she couldn't pull herself away from it. When his lips finally touched hers, she stiffened as the wave of panic she'd felt before, like a crippling force, became the thing that propelled her to action.

Jo moved her head back, separating their lips as she stared in wide-eyed alarm at the man whose gray eyes opened in surprise before shuttering with regret.

"Jo, I...I'm sorry. I shouldn't have done that," he apologized.

"Okay," Jo replied simply, turning back to rinsing the dishes. Daniel resumed his post by the sink and continued to wash the dishes. This time, the silence between them was wrought with tension and unspoken words.

"My husband and my son died in a car crash last year," she heard the words leave her mouth as a wave of pain passed through her.

"I'm sorry to hear that. I can't imagine how devastating that must have been for you," he sympathized.

Jo looked up at the man and gave him a wry smile. "I can't get into a relationship right now...with anyone...because I...I—"

"Hey, it's okay. You don't have to explain. I get it. You need more time to deal with the loss and what I did was not cool," he rushed to say.

Jo gave him a small smile. "I hope we can remain friends, though," she offered.

"Of course," he agreed. "That's what you need right now."

Just then, a knock sounded on the metal doors, startling Jo. She whirled her head around at the same time as Daniel to see Andrea, Cora, and Marg stepping into the kitchen.

"Hey, Jo, want to go to The Anchor with us?"

Chapter Seventeen

"What are you guys going on about?" Jo asked, buying herself time to calm her beating heart. She had been surprised the moment they pushed the kitchen doors open, and as the guilt of what happened earlier seeped in, she tried to distance herself from Daniel by going to stand by the prep table.

"We're going to The Anchor for drinks. Come with us. It'll be fun."

"I can't just leave. I'm in the middle of cleaning up. Today was a very busy day for the restaurant," she explained.

"It's okay. You can go. I've got this covered," Daniel assured her.

She looked over at him with concern. "Are you sure? I don't feel comfortable leaving all this work on you."

"Jo, seriously, it's fine. You did great today, and besides, there isn't a lot left to do here," he continued, gesturing to the few plates left on the counter. She still didn't feel comfortable leaving him alone to clean up the rest of the mess, considering that the pots still needed to be washed, but instead of calling his attention to that, she turned to her sisters.

"What about Mom? Who's staying with her?"

"Jules offered to keep an eye on her since she'll be home," Cora replied.

"Oh," Jo returned.

As if sensing her hesitation, Andrea chimed in. "Tell you what. Why don't we help with the dishes and then we can go? I'm sensing you won't feel comfortable if we leave Daniel to finish up."

Jo gave her sister a small smile.

Just like that, the women joined in to help get the kitchen spick and span.

"So, I'll see you tomorrow," Daniel directed his words to Jo the moment the group exited the restaurant.

Jo looked up at him and gave him a half smile before averting her eyes. "See you tomorrow," she replied before walking away with her sisters and Marg.

When the four women entered the bar, it was already packed, as it seemed tonight was one of those nights that everyone chose for social outings. It didn't take long for them to get seated, though. As soon as the bartender and owner, Jack Fletcher, a former high school friend, saw them, he took an extra table and chairs from the back for them to use. Although they were set up close to the doors that led to the restrooms, it was better than having to wait half an hour to an hour for a spot for their group.

"Thanks, Jake. I appreciate this." Cora smiled up at the bald-headed, muscled man that looked like he could pass for a wrestler.

"Anything for you, Cora." He beamed warmly at her. "Anything for the Triple H and their friends," he added, giving everyone at the table a toothy grin and a wink before walking off to get their drinks.

"So, whose brilliant idea was it to come here tonight?" Jo asked, looking around the table at her sisters and friend.

Cora and Marg pointed to Andrea, who was already sipping on a drink she swiped from the bar.

"We all need to live a little," Andrea shot, with a slight shrug and a smirk on her lips. "We've all had a crazy week. We deserve this."

The others nodded in agreement, each thinking back on what had transpired during the week.

Just then, Jack returned with their drinks. Everyone ordered a cocktail except for Marg, who wasn't much of a drinker and had opted to be the designated driver. After thanking Jack, the women took sips of their drink, sighing in contentment. Jo savored the sweet fruity taste of her sangria that evened out the bitter taste of the red wine. It was one of her favorites to drink, but she still had to pace herself, or she could succumb to the alcohol content quite quickly. The drink was enough for her to make up her mind that she had made the right choice to come out with her sisters.

"This drink right here is giving me life," Andrea gushed as she continued to sip on her mixed drink. "Marg, sweetie, you're missing out."

Marg gave her a rueful smile before ducking her head to take a sip of the sparkling water.

"Why don't you drink, though?" Jo found herself asking out of curiosity. "Is it a religious thing?"

By the way Marg's eyes widened into saucers behind her glasses, and her lips quivered, Jo regretted the question. She didn't want the woman to feel uncomfortable on account of her questioning. She liked Marg. They had all become fast friends with the woman. So much, in fact, that she knew Cora and Andrea had already considered her to be a part of the family. Jo was fast leaning toward that as well. Still, there was so much about the woman with the bubbly smile and personality that could brighten up anyone's day that she didn't know and had found herself wondering about on many occasions.

"I don't drink because alcohol was one of my ex-husband's vices, and I saw what it did to him," she spoke softly, keeping her gaze down and away from the others.

"Oh," Andrea gave out in surprise. "I didn't know you were married."

Marg brought her shoulders up to her chin before dropping them again, her lips drawn in a thin line followed the action. "It was a long time ago," she returned nonchalantly. It didn't hide the pain Jo had ciphered in her eyes, though.

Jo's heart prickled with sympathy for her, knowing how it felt to have so much to share but holding back out of fear. She hoped the woman would be able to get the courage to one day share her pain with others so that she didn't have to carry the burden by herself.

Andrea reached over and grasped Marg's hand that was resting on the tabletop and gave it a squeeze of reassurance. "If you ever need to talk, you can talk to us," she offered. "I promise, we won't judge. Right guys?" Andrea turned her head to look at her sisters, communicating with her light blue eyes the need for them to jump in and back up.

Cora simply nodded her response, reaching over to place her hand on the one Andrea had over Marg's.

"She's right," Jo agreed as she placed her hand over their connected ones. "We all have our own closets full of skeletons, some more than others, but it pays to have someone in your corner when the going gets tough," she encouraged.

Marg's lips curved into a grateful grin. "Thanks, guys. I'm happy for your friendship," she expressed.

The others gave her another reassuring smile.

"How's your grandmother, by the way?" Jo asked, remembering the last time they'd spoken about her.

Marg's expression dulled once more, but she responded.

"Grandma is doing much better, but the possibility of her living past the end of this year is ..." the woman released a soft breath as her eyes glazed over.

"Mom has ALS."

Jo looked over at Cora, surprised but pleased that she revealed their mother's condition to the woman who sat with them, agonizing over her family.

"We don't know how long we'll have with her. The doctors say based on their findings it could be anywhere from three months to possibly one year, two tops," Cora continued to say.

Andrea jumped in, "We know what you're going through, Marg, and we know it can't be easy to be around your grandmother day in, day out, knowing that her life is coming to a close."

"But it helps to have friends, people who know what you're going through and can offer some support to you," Jo finished, reaching out to grasp the woman's hand in hers again.

"I didn't know Becky was sick. I'm so sorry to hear that," Marg spoke up, expressing her sympathies. "I can't imagine how you all must feel, considering how much you've lost recently."

Jo gave the woman a small smile as her mind raced to other memories. Feeling the weight of them, she removed her hand from Marg's and reached for her beverage. Instead of sipping the liquid, she tipped the glass and took a big gulp.

The others grabbed their own drinks and put them to their lips, each lost in their thoughts.

"All right, no more gloomy talk for the rest of the night. We came here to have fun, to let off some steam... Let's have fun." Andrea downed the liquid in the single-shot glass in one go before rising from the table, eyes glinting with mischief. "Let's dance," she invited the others.

Jo looked at her sister as if she was crazy. "What?" she

asked, voicing her surprise. Even though the bar had music belting from the speakers, it wasn't music for dancing. In fact, the bar wasn't necessarily arranged in a way to incorporate the activity. In fact, the establishment was part bar, part diner, distinguished by one area being on a higher platform. Currently, they were sitting in the sunken area that was the diner, and all the booths were occupied. However, that didn't seem to perturb Andrea, who was already swaying in rhythm with the beat.

"Come on, guys, it's fun," she implored her sisters and friend to join her even as they continued to look at her dumbstruck.

Cora slid out of her seat to join her sister, to Jo's horror. She noticed the two were getting curious looks from the other patrons, but that didn't deter them.

Jo looked over at Marg, who looked conflicted. Feeling the urge to let loose like her sisters and enjoy herself, Jo downed the rest of her drink for liquid courage before sliding off her seat to join them.

"Yeah. That's what I'm talking about. Triple H is back!"

The sisters laughed as they basked in the encouragement from Jack. Soon, a few more patrons sidled out of their seats to start swaying to the music.

Jo felt light and free. She hadn't felt this way in a long time, and she didn't want it to end. Turning to their table, she beckoned to Marg with her fingers. The woman shook her head, but Jo felt a wave of determination to get the woman up to have some fun.

"Come on. It's fun," she mouthed.

Marg chewed her bottom lip as her gaze darted around the establishment nervously. Slowly, she got up from her seat and went to join the trio.

As time went on, more people gained the confidence to

move from their seats and join in the festivities. The once quiet bar was now filled with music, laughter, and mingling. The sisters found themselves at the head of the train dancing to the song "Macarena." By the time they exited the bar, they were tired but still buzzing from how much fun they had.

Chapter Eighteen

Jo stretched languidly as the first few notes from her alarm reached her ears. She slowly opened her eyes to see the first signs of the morning already seeping through the sheer curtains. Reaching over to the bedside table, she quickly clicked the snooze button before rolling back over with a sigh. She was still tired from the outing last night, but she couldn't sleep in as she wanted to go into the restaurant to do some pre-preparation for the lunch and dinner menus. The family was having a get-together later, so she wouldn't be able to work at the restaurant. It was the next best option to ensure that Daniel didn't have his hands too full.

As her thoughts shifted to the six-foot one-inch-tall French chef, she couldn't help the slight flutter that disturbed her stomach. The kiss had caught her by surprise, but she would've been lying if she'd said it wasn't pleasant. She hadn't been kissed in a long time, and yet that one kiss had awoken something inside her that she'd thought had been buried with her husband. However, it wasn't something that she could entertain. The kiss had moved from feeling pleasant to her feeling as though she was betraying the memory of Charles, the one man she'd ever loved, and Nicholas, the second love of her life. Allowing Daniel to kiss her felt as if she was letting go of them and the memory of the life they had. She wasn't ready to do that. Spending too much time contemplating the kiss and the man who delivered it was dangerous, and she needed to get a move on with the day.

Jo swung her legs over the side of her bed and stood to make her way to the bathroom to freshen up. When she was finished, she donned simple denim pants and a white T-shirt before making her way downstairs. It was still early, and she was sure her sisters were still passed out from how much fun they had last night and how much they drank. A smile decorated her lips as memories of their activities came to mind. They had truly been the life of the party, so much so that the patrons had started chanting "Triple H."

When she finally made it to the restaurant, Jo keyed in the code before pushing the back door open. She made her way to the kitchen to start preparations. When she was satisfied with everything, she'd made a note for Daniel to let him know she wouldn't be in for the day.

Jo exited the restaurant the same way she'd entered and made the ten-minute trek back to the main house. She found her niece sitting out on the front porch, gaze trained on the book in her hands. Jules was either too engrossed or just couldn't bother to notice Jo's assent when she came to stand directly before her.

"It's that good, huh?" she asked, bringing Jules's attention to her.

Jules looked up, her blue eyes registering surprise to see Jo. "I didn't hear you walk up," she spoke, a polite smile finding its way onto her face.

"I noticed," Jo returned. "I guess this must be one of those page-turners that draw you in, and nothing else matters," she continued, gesturing to the book in her niece's hands.

"Oh, this?" Jules asked, making a face as she flipped it so Jo had a better look at the cover. "It's more like compulsory reading for a test you never planned on taking." She sighed.

Jo felt sorry for the young woman who looked on the verge of having a meltdown. She remembered what it was like being pregnant for the first time. Even though she was a bit older than her niece and had the support of an attentive and loving husband, she had felt the raw fear of the unknown, and doubts had seeped in on whether or not she would be a good mother. In the end, it turned out great. Her niece's case, however, was a bit more delicate in nature. She knew Cora was struggling to accept this, and so it had put a strain on the two's relationship, and she could only imagine how guarded Jules felt she needed to be with the rest of the family that hadn't really been an integral part of her life for so many years.

"Want to go somewhere with me?" Jo invited.

Jules's brows furrowed as she waited for her aunt to explain further.

"I want to take you out on the water in your grandpa's boat. It'll be fun, I promise," she informed her.

"Okay," Jules agreed.

"Great, let's go change into bathing suits and sundresses."

The young woman nodded her agreement and placed the book on the small table by the side before rising to her feet and following Jo inside.

"Where are the others?" Jo asked the minute they stepped in, and she realized that the house was empty.

"Aunt Drea is by the inn helping Ms. Marg out, and Mom took Grandma into town to do some shopping."

"That's good. It gives us some time to just have fun," Jo expressed with a twinkle.

Jules smiled back but said nothing.

When the two had donned their respective outfits, they left out the back door and made their way down the patio, past the flower garden, and through the wall of trees hiding the dock from view.

Her father's old boat was safely moored under the bottom of the two-story dock. The boat had been refurbished until it looked brand new, sporting the name *Silver Bullet,* a name heavy with sentimentality. She smiled happily as memories of the many times her father would take her and her sisters out to the Camano Island State Park to trek the forest loop trail there or go fishing or crab hunting in the Saratoga Passage. Those had been some very fun memories of them all being together as a family. Turning to her niece, she asked, "Ready to have some fun?"

Jules's face registered anything but enthusiasm.

Jo stood at the wheel, navigating the *Silver Bullet* as the boat sliced through the clear blue waters, as the steady chug of the engine drove the vessel forward. A foamy stream of bubbles formed a clear path behind it. Jo looked over her shoulder at her niece, who sat in the back, sunglasses covering her eyes, her head slightly resting against the back of the seat. Jo couldn't tell if she was awake, taking in the scenery, or asleep. She released the wheel, giving it some slack causing the boat to swerve a little, sending up a spray of water that hit them both. Jules sat up and removed her shades. Jo smiled at her.

"Wanna try steering?" she invited. After a few seconds of silent contemplation, Jules rose from her position to join her aunt.

"Here, hold the wheel," she instructed her niece, scooting over to give her room.

"What do I do?" Jules asked as she gripped the wheel until her knuckles were white.

"Nothing really," Jo replied. "Just imagine you're driving a car. This is the throttle. It kind of operates like a brake, but not entirely. If you want the boat to stop completely, you have to push this button in the middle— the kill switch," she gave a few basic instructions.

"Okay." Jules nodded while she listened. "Sounds pretty straightforward. Well, let's pray I don't send us crashing into some sharp rocks, you know, considering this is my first time without actual lessons," she finished indifferently.

Jo laughed at her niece's sarcasm. The ride to the south side of the islands where she and her sisters had swum the last time they took the boat out was uneventful, and suffice to say, Jules did well driving the boat there and mooring it in the direction of her aunt.

Removing their sundresses, the two women took turns diving off the helm of the boat into the cool water that enveloped them as soon as they broke the surface. They swam back and forth for short distances before flipping onto their backs, the salinity of the water providing the necessary buoyancy to keep them afloat.

After some time of enjoying the water, the two climbed back on deck.

"What's on your mind?" Jo asked. They sat there for another half an hour just lazing on the deck, soaking up the sun and taking in the panoramic view of the endless skies that dipped to meet the endless ocean in the distance.

Jules didn't readily answer her. She looked over to make sure she wasn't asleep, but the sunglasses were once more, making it difficult for her to determine that.

Jo turned away from her niece to follow the flight of a few birds, their black wings flapping endlessly against invisible currents as they seemed to soar even higher as if trying to break the barrier of the blue sky. If she were a painter, this would have been the perfect scenery to paint, in her opinion.

She heard a slight ruffling beside her before she saw her niece raise up until she was in a seated position. Jules drew her legs up to her chest and wrapped her arms around them before releasing a long, tired sigh.

"I feel like such a screwup," she confessed softly.

Jo quickly sat up and turned fully to her niece.

"My whole life is messed up now because of this... this..." The young woman sighed sadly, not able to get out the words she wanted to say.

Jo's heart constricted at the pain Jules was experiencing. She waited for her to continue.

"Everyone looks at me like I am the biggest screwup, and Mom..."

Jo reached over to touch Jules's arm at the sound of her sniffles from under her arms. She scooted closer to rest her hand over her niece's shoulders and brought her to her side, offering all the support she could.

"I had everything planned out perfectly, Aunt Jo. I was going to go to college, finish my journalism degree and work for the New York Times, but now, none of that matters because I have thi-th-this baby growing inside of me," she continued with a mirthless laugh before she gulped back another sob.

"You can still have those things, Jules," Jo spoke up reassuringly. "Just because you made one mistake doesn't mean you have to give up on your dreams. It just means that you'll have to fight harder this time around."

Jo reached over with her free hand to lift her face so she could stare into her eyes as she continued. Jules's tear-stained blue eyes, which were now red around the edges, stared back at her with anguish.

"You need to know that your mom loves you very much and only wants what's best for you. In the end, she's only ever wanted you girls to be the best version of yourselves. You'll have to meet her halfway, though. Talk to her. Let her in," Jo implored.

Jo sighed, pulling her head away from her aunt and staring

out across the waters. "I tried, Aunt Jo, but Mom doesn't get that this is my decision to make and not hers— even... even if it's the hard choice," she whispered at the end.

"So, I take it you have chosen to keep the baby?" Jo asked cautiously.

Jules nodded in response.

"That is a good choice," she agreed, reinforcing her niece's decision. "But even if you had chosen the alternative, it would still be your choice."

Jules looked sideways at her aunt and gave her a grateful smile.

"We're all here for you, Jules. We've got your back, and this baby that you're carrying will receive nothing but love and warmth when he or she arrives," Jo assured her, giving her a light nudge against her shoulder.

"Thanks, Aunt Jo. You don't know how much I needed to hear those words right now."

Jo stood to her feet, bringing her niece into an embrace, holding her to her chest, and willing her to feel the love and security that she needed.

Chapter Nineteen

"Looks like the party started without us," Jo remarked the moment the house came into view.

A number of people could be seen under the patio. She could smell the faint scent of grilled meat which became even more apparent the closer they got to the house. She could also make out the group of people out on the patio. Cora and Jamie stood by the charcoal barrel grill. Jamie appeared to be flipping whatever meat he had on the grill while being entertained by whatever Cora was whispering to him as he threw his head back to laugh.

Andrea stood to the far corner with the firefighter, Donny, that seemed to be frequenting these family get-togethers as much as Jamie. She was happy that her sisters were both taking a chance at love again. No one deserved it as much as them, especially Andrea. She also saw Uncle Luke, her mom, and Aunt Maria sitting in wicker chairs, conversing among themselves, and laughing.

Cora, who was the first to notice their approach whispered something to Jamie before walking a few steps down the path.

"Hey," she greeted. "I was starting to worry about you guys. Where were you?" Even though the question was thrown out to them both, she noted how intensely Cora was staring at her daughter.

"I thought we needed a little aunt and niece time away from everything to just bond, so I took her out on the water," Jo jumped in.

"Okay. That's... that's great," Cora replied, her tone unsure. "Did you enjoy the trip, Jules," she asked, a small smile on her lips as she waited for a response.

"I did. It was a wonderful experience," Jules replied simply.

After a minute of the trio standing awkwardly, Jules finally spoke. "I'm going to take a shower, and then I'll head back to this shindig." Jo needed to go take a shower, too, after spending the whole day out at sea and having only done a quick rinse off with the jug of water she'd brought, but she decided she'd greet the others before doing so.

"Okay, sweetie. We'll talk later." Jules gave her mother a small smile before heading for the house. Cora watched her until she was out of sight before turning back to her little sister.

Jo looked at her sister and knew that she was in turmoil. Her eyes were filled with anguish, and her lips were folded in on each other. "I blew it, Jo. My daughter can't even bear to look me in the eyes when we're talking because instead of listening to her and trying to support her decision, I decided to play hardball. Now I don't know what's going on in her head because she just won't talk to me about it."

Jo reached out and ran a hand over her sister's arm. "You have to give her time and space, but you also have to demonstrate that you're here for her, Cora," Jo encouraged her sister. "I think her greatest fear in this whole ordeal is that her decision to keep the baby will be something that you hold over her head for the rest of her life."

Cora's gray-blue eyes widened in surprise. "Is that what she thought I meant by time is running out for her to make a choice?" she asked incredulously before her face crumpled into hurt and trepidation. "Oh my god, Jo. I would never ask her to..." She sighed in frustration.

Cora ran her fingers through her brown hair as the implication of her words and how much it had hurt her daughter hit her full force. "I only meant that she needed to decide if she wanted to start college this year or defer for a year, but time was running out to make the decision," she turned, trying to clarify to Jo.

Jo gave her a sympathetic look. She knew how words could be misconstrued in the heat of the moment and the damage it was able to cause if the light wasn't shed on the misunderstanding.

"I have to go talk to her," Cora spoke with urgency. Jo simply nodded in understanding. At that, Cora turned on her heels and made her way inside the house.

"Hey, what was that about?"

Jo looked around to see Andrea coming over to where she stood. "Just something Cora needs to clear up with her daughter so that their relationship can mend," she informed her.

"Oh, well, I hope it works out," Andrea spoke with hope. "Jules is going to need her mother for this pregnancy, and Cora won't be able to focus on her budding romance with Jamie if she's at loggerheads with her daughter."

"Speaking of romance," Jo injected, a gleam forming in her eyes. "What's up with you and Mr. Firefighter lately?"

She noted the sudden tint to her sister's cheeks as she quickly ducked her head. "Donny's great," she said shyly. "He's a gentleman, kind, sweet, and fiercely loyal."

"Those are all good qualities to want in a man," Jo noted. "So why does there seem to be hesitation on your part?"

"He is all of the above and more," Andrea confirmed before

sighing. "It's just that I don't know, his son, well, one of them doesn't like me very much or the idea of us getting into a relationship, and as much as I like him, I just don't want to get into the way of his bond with his son," she expressed her fear.

Jo looked pointedly at her sister. "Does he make you happy?"

Andrea took a little time to think about it before a big smile broke on her lips. "He does," she said. "He's always finding ways to make me feel special."

"Then that's all that matters," Jo affirmed. "Our children have their own lives to live. It's only natural that we should be given the same freedom to make our own choices. Don't worry. He'll come around. Just focus on what you have with Donny and block out the chatter."

"When did you get so wise?" Andrea joked as she bumped her sister's shoulder.

Jo laughed. "It's from watching countless Kung Fu movies with Charles. They made me very sage," she said in the gravest voice she could muster.

"Seems like I'll have to start watching more of those then," Andrea returned. The two continued talking as they made their way over to the others.

"Hi, sweetie," Becky greeted her daughter, who bent and gave her a kiss on the cheek.

Jo moved on to greet her uncle and his wife before reaching the tall, muscular, blond-haired man that was her sister's plus one at the gathering. "Donny, it's a pleasure to see you again," she spoke sincerely as she leaned in to give him a light hug.

"It's nice to see you again, Jo," the man replied, hitting her with a dazzling smile.

"Orders up," she heard Jamie call out from the far end where he stood in front of the grill.

"I'll go get the buns," her mother said, rising from the chair to make her way inside.

"I'll go get them," Jo offered, but her mother waved her off. Realizing she'd be fighting a losing battle, she allowed her mother to go get buns.

Cora and Jules came out of the house a short while after their mother went in and joined the party. From the looks on their faces, she could tell that they had made up. Jo was happy for them. They had a long journey ahead of them, but at least they had each other.

"Buns are here," Becky called from the porch steps, holding up the two bags. The group cheered her on.

"Let me go help Jamie put these sandwiches together," Uncle Luke informed the group, rising from his seat and heading toward the grill.

Becky was only a foot behind him when her foot snagged on something, and she went tumbling to the ground. When she cried out in surprise at her sudden falling, Uncle Luke turned and reached out to her, but it was too late. She'd already made contact with the concrete. She cried out in pain and shock at the impact.

Jo's heart clenched in horror at the whole incident, and she stood frozen as her limbs tried to catch up with the command from her brain to move.

"Where does it hurt?" she heard Uncle Luke ask her mother as he gently helped her up with a hand on her back. Jo's feet started moving, taking her closer to the scene.

"M-my h-h...hand," she heard Becky strain to say, cradling her right arm in the left.

"We need to get her to the hospital," Cora said with urgency.

"I'll take her in the Jeep. The girls can ride with me," Uncle Luke said. "I'll call Tessa to let her know what happened and that we're on our way."

The next few minutes were a flurry of activities. Jamie had lifted Becky into the back of the Jeep with Jo and Andrea on either side of her. Cora was up front with Uncle Luke. As soon as everyone was secure, the vehicle peeled out of the property, and in less than fifteen minutes, they were at the entrance of the Whidbey Island Public Hospital. Tessa and a few other nurses were already awaiting their arrival. They sat Becky in a wheelchair and wheeled her away, leaving the family in the waiting area.

Half an hour later, and still, no news had come about their mother. Jo's heartbeat pounded in her ear, any louder, and she suspected everyone would be able to hear it, not just her. She sat with the back of her head against the wall. Cora stood, pacing back and forth, and Andrea sat in the opposite chair with her hands around her body as she chewed on her bottom lip nervously. Uncle Luke was the only one who seemed the calmest as he stood by the far wall with his hands over his chest, watching the time on the clock.

An hour later, Tessa came into the room.

"Is she okay?" Cora asked immediately.

Tessa gave the family a reassuring smile. "Aunt Becky is fine," she reassured them.

Everyone released an audible sigh of relief.

"She, however, suffered a hairline fracture of her forearm. It's minor, so she won't need surgery. However, she will have to wear a cast for the next six weeks while it heals," she explained to them. "The doctor will come and fill you in on all the details. I just thought it best that I gave you the news first."

"Thanks, Tess," Andrea said, going over to hug their cousin tightly. The other two did the same.

After the doctor came and practically went over all that Tessa had already told them, they were allowed to go see her. Becky lay on the narrow hospital bed with a white cast that ran from her elbow to the base of her fingers, completely encasing it.

"Hey," she greeted as soon as her daughters stepped through the door.

They each went over and hugged her tightly. "You gave us a scare, Mom, but we're glad you're okay."

"I'm sorry I did that," she apologized.

"It wasn't your fault, Mom," Jo spoke up. "It could have happened to any one of us. We're just glad that you're okay." The others nodded in agreement.

"My babies," Becky broke down, which caused them to break down as well as they all rushed to hug her, taking care not to touch her cast.

After getting the prescription and signing the release forms, they left the hospital and headed home.

Chapter Twenty

"I'm taking Mom up to her room to get her settled in," Andrea informed her sisters as soon as they walked through the front door.

"Okay," the other two sisters agreed.

As they moved from the foyer toward the stairs, Jo and Cora watched as Andrea carefully guided their mother up the stairs, a firm hand under her casted arm to prevent it from hitting against the wall.

Cora released a heavy sigh as she headed toward the back door, and Jo followed suit.

"Hi, sweetie. Luke told me what the doctors said. Where is she?" Aunt Maria rose from the chair she'd been sitting in to come and hug Cora, then Jo.

"Andrea took her to her room to get some rest," Jo told her.

"Okay, I'm just going to say hello to her before Luke comes to get me," Aunt Maria informed them before heading inside.

"Hey."

Jo looked over the railing to see Jamie looking up at Cora with a mixture of affection and concern.

"Hey," she heard Cora answer with a smile on her lips.

"I'm gonna head inside and start washing up," she said to Cora, wanting to give the two some privacy.

"All right. I'll be in shortly to help," Cora turned to say.

Jo gave her a slight nod before heading inside. She headed for the kitchen and started transferring the leftovers to sealed containers before placing them in the refrigerator. After rinsing the gravy from the dishes, she placed them in the dishwasher and then started it. She rested her back against the counter and her head against the cabinets before releasing a long sigh.

"Tired?"

Jo lowered her head to her sister, who had just walked into the kitchen, giving her a sympathetic look. "More like drained," she confessed as her shoulders fell.

"Maybe after we're finished here, we can sit out on the porch and unwind," Cora suggested, moving to take up a dishtowel.

"That's not a bad idea," Jo agreed, reaching for a towel, and joining her sister by the dishwasher that had chimed, indicating the cycle was done. "Where's Jamie?"

"He just left. He has an early morning tomorrow. He's driving to Seattle to look at a job," Cora told her.

"You two are getting really serious, huh?" Jo asked, giving her a knowing smile as she took the dish she offered and began drying it.

An instant grin painted Cora's lips. "I don't know, Jo... it's like I've never felt this way about anyone, not even with Joel when we first started dating. It's exhilarating... it's, it's scary." She chuckled at the last sentence. "But it's also freeing. With Jamie, I can be myself without fear of judgment, and he makes me want to... I don't know. It's hard to explain."

"It sounds like you're in love with him, Cora," Jo offered.

Cora stopped drying the plate she held in her hand to look

out at the darkness behind the windowpanes. After a good ten seconds, her face softened. "I think I am," she confirmed, still looking outside. "Oh, wow!" she exclaimed, startling Jo. "I'm in love with Jamie Hillier."

"I'm happy for you, Cora," Jo responded with a sincere smile. "You deserve to be happy. You deserve all of it and so much more."

With her support, Cora pulled Jo into a tight hug. "Thanks, Jo," she spoke against her temple. At this, Jo's smile broadened.

"What are we celebrating?"

The two sisters pulled apart and turned to Andrea, who looked at them with a quizzical yet excited expression.

"Cora's in love," Jo blurted.

Andrea's face lit up even more from the news. "Finally! I was wondering how long it would take you to admit that little fact… that you burn for the man." She smirked, a mischievous glint in her light blue eyes.

Cora stuck her tongue out at her before breaking out into laughter. The other two joined in the euphoria.

After the laughter had died down, Jo asked, "How is Mom doing?"

"She's okay. I guess the pain meds are doing their job because she's not feeling any pain. She is adamant though that eight is too early for her to go to bed," Andrea told them.

The mood from earlier dampened a bit with the mention of their mother.

"I'll go check on her," Jo piped up.

"All right. I'll set up for our nightcap," Cora informed her.

Andrea's brows furrowed in confusion.

"We're planning to have a small relaxing session on the porch," Jo answered the unasked question.

"Oh, that's a great idea," she endorsed.

Jo nodded before making her way to the stairs

"Come in," she heard her mother call out the minute she rapped on the door.

Jo slowly opened it and stepped inside. Her mother, who was propped up with pillows against the headboard, smiled invitingly at her. "Hi, how are you feeling?" she asked, making her way over to stand by the bedside.

"Well, it could have been worse," Becky replied, slightly raising the arm with the cast that rested on her tummy.

Jo gave her a sympathetic smile.

"Sweetie, what's wrong?" Becky asked with concern as Jo stood looking down at her with angst, her eyes bright with unshed tears.

"Nothing, nothing," Jo rushed to say.

"Jo." Becky sighed. "I know something is bothering you, sweetie. I can see it on your face." She drew herself further up into a sitting position and patted the space beside her.

Immediately, Jo sat on the edge of the bed, then scooted further up until she was tucked into her mother's side. Becky used her good hand to draw Jo's head down until it nestled into the crook of her neck. The two didn't speak for a while.

"I love you, Mom," Jo murmured, breaking the silence.

"I know you do, sweetie," Becky spoke knowingly. "I love you too."

Jo lifted her head and turned to her mother. Becky turned her head to look at her. "I know I haven't said it, but I'm really glad that you're my mom. I appreciate how patient you were with me even when I was going through those years of rebellion after Cora and Drea left. I know I was being a brat." Jo winced at the memory. "If I hadn't been so stubborn and blinded by the hurt and resentment I felt toward everyone, I would have realized that everything you did was for my benefit." She smiled a sad smile as her mind brought up images of her teenage years.

Jo remembered how she would blow up at every suggestion Becky made, especially when it concerned her staying in Oak

Harbor. She had thought her mother wanted her to stay for all the selfish reasons her dad had wanted her to stay, but the more she thought about it, the more she realized Becky had only ever wanted what was best for her.

She felt the warmth from her mother's palm seep through her cheek where it now rested, and she turned her eyes to look into the brown ones that were a mirror of her own. Jo gave her a grateful smile.

"I am so proud of the woman you've become, Josephine. You and your sisters chose your own paths. It was meant to be that way. I am just happy that I got to live long enough to see the wonderful, brave, selfless woman you have grown to become, and I get to share in that. I couldn't ask for anything else."

Jo felt a tear roll down her cheek at her mother's speech. Becky used the pad of her thumb to wipe away the remnants. "It means a lot to hear you say that." She breathed out, wrapping her arms around her mother's shoulders.

After their moment, Jo helped her mother get settled once more and headed downstairs to the porch. She walked to the side that overlooked the harbor.

"We were about to send the search party to come to get you," Andrea said, handing her a glass of wine.

Jo took a sip of the sweet yet tangy-flavored wine as she sat in the wicker chair situated between her sisters. "I had a heart-to-heart with Mom," she revealed.

The two sisters looked over at her, the moonlight bathing their faces in its bright aura.

"How did that go?" Cora asked cautiously.

Jo turned to her with a big grin. "It went great. It's funny how years of living away from this place and then coming back have put things into perspective in a way I never imagined," she mused, taking another sip from her glass.

The sisters nodded their agreement but chose not to add

anything, each lost in their own thoughts as they stared out across the night sky into the vast ocean illuminated by the moonlight, navy blue waves lapping at each other.

"I've decided that I'm staying in Oak Harbor permanently," Jo confessed to the silence that surrounded them.

"Oh, wow, that's wonderful news," Andrea expressed happily. She reached over and wrapped her fingers around Jo's hand and gave it a firm squeeze.

"I'm happy you decided to stay, Jo." Cora looked at her sister with a genuine smile.

"Yeah, I thought about it, and there isn't anything left in Tacoma for me. Tracy and Josh are okay and getting ready to start their lives together and the restaurant... I don't know. As much as I loved working there, it just hasn't been the same since."

She felt Cora's warm hand on her other arm, running up and down, and she turned to give her a grateful smile before staring out at the ocean once more.

"There isn't anything to go back to," she admitted with finality. "But here... here I have everything that I need." Jo looked back and forth at her sisters as she emphasized the point. "I have two sisters that I know now would do anything for me, and the empty space that has been in my heart since our separation is finally healing. And Mom...God, I've missed Mom... I'm so happy that I got to talk to her and apologize before it's too late."

A small, melancholic smirk graced her lips as she thought about all she'd been through up until this point. "So much has been taken from me in the past year, but I've also gained so much, and I'm truly, truly thankful."

The hands that rested against hers gave her another firm squeeze. "I almost forgot. I didn't remember seeing Jules when we got home. Where is she?"

"Oh, Jamie, Nikki, and Tracy came to pick her up to go watch a movie," Cora answered.

"That's nice. I'm glad our kids are getting along so well with their cousins," Jo said appreciatively. "Wait, you said Tracy—"

"Kerry's daughter Tracy," Cora jumped in to clarify.

Jo nodded in acknowledgment before emptying the contents of her glass.

"It would have been nice if they got the opportunity to grow up around each other but watching them become fast friends and so close is really something beautiful," Andrea expressed. All three sisters exchanged knowing looks.

"So, you and Jules," Jo spoke, looking over at her sister, the unspoken question and invitation for Cora to tell them what transpired after her talk with Jules.

"We're making progress," Cora revealed, a small smile gracing her lips.

Jo and Andrea returned her smile, relieved that they were working on their relationship.

"She's decided to defer for a year to put all of her energy into making sure she delivers a healthy baby. She's going to stay here, too, so that I can help her," Cora revealed.

"Great, now you won't have to worry about her as much," Andrea spoke up.

Cora nodded in agreement. "I remember how hard it was when I first got pregnant with Erin. I wished I had Mom to walk me through the steps, to tell me that everything was going to be okay."

"I know what you mean," Andrea added. "It was the scariest experience of my whole life being pregnant with Aurora and alone, but Jules... she's lucky. She has you, us, and Mom so that she doesn't have to do it by herself."

Cora gave her sisters an appreciative smile, but as her

thoughts shifted, her expression changed. With furrowed brows and a contemplative look, she turned to them. "I really don't want to push her, but I wish she would tell me something about the father of her baby."

Chapter Twenty-One

Jo woke up with a start, feeling overwhelmed by the thoughts flooding into her mind. She sat up in the bed and scooted further up to rest her back against the headboard. Her fingers went up to touch her lips, almost as if in a trance.

"It was so real," she spoke with incredulity. She couldn't believe that she dreamed about Daniel— Daniel kissing her again, nonetheless. This was the second night in a row that her mind had rested on him.

She hadn't even gone to bed last night with him on her mind. The last thing she remembered was telling her sisters how much she had missed Charles and them telling her that with time it would get easier. Yet here she was dreaming about another man.

Why did he have to kiss me? She needed to see him.

Swinging her feet over the side of the bed, she got up and went to the bathroom to do her routine and get the day started. Donning some skinny jeans and a plain white tee, she tied her hair into a high ponytail and headed over to the Bistro.

"Hi, Suzie," she greeted the bubbly young woman. "Is Daniel in?"

"Hi, Jo," she greeted back. "No, today is the chef's day off. We're actually serving deli items from the kiosk for today," the young woman informed her.

"Oh," Jo replied, disappointed. "That's a bummer. I really need to see him today. I guess I'll wait until tomorrow then. See you later, Suzie," she said, waving goodbye.

"Bye, Jo." Suzie waved. "Um, Jo," Suzie called out just as Jo was about to step through the door.

"Yes?" Jo asked, turning to face the girl.

"The chef's phone number and address are in the sign-in book if you really need to see him today," she said. "It's at the front."

"Thanks, Suzie," Jo returned with a grateful smile, heading for the kitchen where the book was kept.

After inputting the information into her phone, she made the ten-minute walk back to the main house to get her keys and the car. The house was still silent when she stepped in, so she decided to send Cora a message as she pulled out of her parking spot. She texted her that she was heading out, and that she would be back later.

"Okay, be safe," her sister replied almost instantly.

"I will, thanks," she sent back.

"All right, Jo. You're not looking for a relationship. You just need him to answer a few questions." She gave herself a pep talk as she drove along the highway on her way to Daniel's home out on Lexington. "You just need to set some boundaries. You didn't do that the last time so now you have to."

As the GPS announced that she was less than six miles away, her panic level went up a notch. Maybe this wasn't such a good idea. She had been known to make rash decisions in the heat of the moment— maybe this was one of them.

By the time the GPS stated that she was only a half mile

away, her heart was beating erratically, and she could feel the perspiration at the nape of her neck even though the air was cool. She chose to focus on the scenery instead of what her body was doing.

She noted that the area was heavily wooded, mainly with evergreens that obscured the properties and blocked the view of Penn Cove. The properties seemed to be few and far and in between.

"In six hundred feet, turn left and continue driving for nine hundred and eighty feet." Jo followed the directives of her GPS and made the left turn onto a dirt road that opened up between the trees and continued driving for another nine hundred feet.

"You have arrived at your destination."

Jo looked out at the property before her in awe. The house had a Cape Cod architecture feel to it with its sharp, slanting roof and French-styled dormer windows. The centered porch protruded away from the house with its gabled roof slightly higher than the rest of the roof and a nice brick chimney just behind one of the slopes. Jo loved the quaintness. She especially loved the a-typical duck egg blue that it was painted in and the small decorative shrubs and wildflowers that lined either side of the porch.

Mustering her courage, she finally stepped out of the car and took the steps up the porch and rang the doorbell. In less than ten seconds, Daniel stood before her with a look of surprise etched on his face.

"Hi," she spoke, cringing at the breathiness of her voice. Clearing her throat, she started again. "I hope I didn't catch you at a bad time," she said with a small, unsure smile.

"You're...here?" Daniel looked at Jo with a level of uncertainty that indicated he wasn't sure if what he was seeing was real.

"I am," Jo confirmed, wringing her fingers.

"You're here," he repeated, this time stating rather than asking. "Would you like to come in?" he asked.

"Um... sure, sure."

Daniel stepped to the side, giving her space to enter the house. She noticed quickly that although the outside made the small home look compact, it was actually very spacious. The room had an open floor plan. She was standing in the living room that was fully furnished with a large beige, eight-seat sectional sofa and an ottoman. A large television was mounted on the opposite wall with an entertainment center housing music speakers and various gadgets. A few feet from the living room was the dining area, and behind that was the kitchen.

"It's so lovely," Jo spoke without thought. "I mean, I love your house. I like the layout and the fact that it's private and surrounded by a forest and water. It's a nature lover's dream getaway spot," she quickly added.

Daniel gave her a knowing smile.

"If you ever think about selling it, count on me to be the first bidder. I mean, I would literally camp out on your lawn until you agreed to sell it to me. That's how much I love it."

Daniel chuckled. "All that for a house, huh?"

The deep, husky sound that came from him caused her heart to skip a beat. "I'm a sucker for natural beauty," Jo replied simply.

"As am I," Daniel replied, staring at her, his gray eyes peering into her soul.

Jo blinked rapidly, trying to clear the fog that took up space in her brain. Her heartbeat had quickened, and there was a flurry of wings in her chest. "Um..." she started, still trying to find enough words to string a proper sentence together from her befuddled thoughts. "Um, I came here to talk to you about something," she finally managed to get out, her voice slightly trembling from the angst she felt.

"Okay, sure," he agreed. "Would you like anything to drink?" he offered.

"Uh, just water, thanks."

"All right." Daniel headed for his kitchen. His head disappeared behind the stainless-steel doors before coming back with bottled water and a can of beer. "Maybe it would be better if we talk outside."

"Yes, sure," Jo agreed, following him out the back door. She fell in love even more with the property as she stared in awe at the beauty of the scene before her.

She had seen glimpses of the water in between the thick barriers the trees created, but from this position, she was treated to a panoramic view of the pristine waters of Penn Cove.

"I knew you would like this," Daniel said from beside her.

"It's beautiful," she whispered reverently.

Daniel's gray eyes crinkled at the corners as his lips curved into a smile while he watched Jo fawn over the view. "What did you want to speak with me about?" he asked after a few minutes of them just staring out across the water. "Let me get you a seat first," he rushed to say before Jo could start talking. He placed the two Adirondack chairs closer to the center of the back porch. After Jo settled in her seat, he lowered himself into the next one.

"You know... you remind me a lot of your father," he spoke after taking a swig of his beer.

Jo looked over at him, surprised by his statement. "How so?" she asked.

"He had the same love that you have for nature. Like you, he loved this property from the moment he lay eyes on it and offered to buy it from me."

Jo grinned in appreciation of the memory of her father Daniel shared with her.

"Sam was a good man. Someone I respected very much." Jo

smiled warmly at this. The two settled into a comfortable silence as they stared out at the water.

"Why did you kiss me?" Jo finally found the nerve to ask. She felt Daniel's gaze on her but kept her head straight.

"Why did you let me kiss you?" he responded at last.

The question threw Jo off guard, and she made the mistake of turning to him. His steel-gray eyes held her prisoner, and as much as she wanted to turn away, she couldn't. Her heart rate quickened when she watched his gaze lower until they were on her lips before returning to her eyes. She felt the warmness in her cheeks and knew she was in trouble. Finally, she found the willpower to look away from his hypnotic stare.

"I told you that my husband and son died in a car accident last year, but I didn't tell you how it happened." Taking in a deep breath, she continued, "Charles, that was my husband's name. He worked for an investment company. He... he um..."

"You don't have to tell me if it's too hard," Charles offered.

"No. I need to get this out so that you understand where I'm coming from."

Daniel nodded his understanding.

"He um used... he made an unauthorized investment using one of his client's funds, and it tanked. He started drinking because his boss found out and demanded that he pay back the money. On the day of the accident, he'd been drinking, and our son Nicholas was with him. He lost control of the vehicle and slammed into a tree. They both died on impact," she recited mechanically to avoid the emotions the memory of them would elicit.

"Oh no, Jo, I'm so sorry. I can't imagine how devastated you must have been," Daniel replied.

Jo turned and gave him a grateful smile for his concern. "I didn't find out about all Charles had been involved in until after the funeral, and I told myself I couldn't let Tracy find out about this. It would devastate her more than she already was and tarnish her father's memory. So, for the better part of a year, I kept this from her. I was forced to tell her recently, and it's created a rift in our relationship. The day after Mom's party, you saw me acting strangely because of what was happening."

Daniel gave her a sympathetic look.

"I'm telling you this because I have a lot of baggage that I have to get through, and the kiss... the kiss was a distraction that I can't entertain right now."

Jo trained her eyes on Daniel, whose unwavering gaze was already on her. "I can't deny that I am attracted to you, but I think it would be best if we take things slow... like really slow and continue being just friends for now."

Daniel nodded in understanding. "I get it," he spoke, giving her a reassuring smile.

The two sat in silence, ruminating on all that had been shared.

"You know," Daniel started slowly, causing Jo to look over at him. "I got divorced because my ex-wife cheated on me, and you are the first woman in more than a decade that I've felt a spark with."

Jo widened her eyes in surprise.

Chapter Twenty-Two

"So, you're telling me you've never been on a date with another woman in the twelve years that you've been divorced?"

"Well, technically... no."

Jo looked Daniel over, unable to comprehend what could have possessed someone to cheat on a man like him. She wondered what was going through his ex-wife's head.

"A friend of mine was going on a date, and he asked me to tag along to keep his date's friend company. We quickly found out we had nothing in common and were actually butting heads a lot. In the end, we just quietly sat at the table staring at said friend and his date, all laughing and flirting, completely oblivious to the fact that we weren't enjoying ourselves."

Jo stared at him in disbelief before bursting into laughter.

"Sure, it's funny now, but back then, it was a mortifying experience. One I vowed to never repeat." Daniel cringed at the memory.

"I can't imagine how awful it must have been," Jo finally tapered her laugh to empathize.

"Yeah," Daniel replied. "It's fine, though. It didn't go anywhere, and at the time, I had my daughter and her future to think about. After what happened between me and her mother, I didn't want to subject her to meeting any random woman with whom the relationship would eventually frazzle out."

"Tell me about your daughter," Jo requested.

At the mention of his daughter, a wide smile broke out on Daniel's face, and Jo found herself smiling too.

"She's the best thing that could have ever happened to me," he spoke, his eyes beaming with the love and affection he felt for his baby girl.

Jo gave him a knowing smile as she bobbed her head.

"Her name is Laura," he supplied. "She's a dental hygienist." He beamed with pride once more.

"How old is she?" Jo found herself becoming very invested in his daughter's life.

"She's twenty-three."

"Wow, that's just... that's mind-blowing," Jo responded, looking at Daniel in wonder. "I remember being that age. I was already a stay-at-home mom, and my life wasn't fully together yet," she confessed.

"That's mind-blowing too," Daniel inserted. "Being a parent... a mother at that age is a phenomenal accomplishment," he said with sincerity. "By what I've seen of your daughter, I gotta say, you did an outstanding job," he complimented.

Jo felt heat rush to her cheeks, and she quickly ducked her head, avoiding his gray eyes that seemed to be able to see straight through her to her very soul. "Thank you," she replied softly, touched by the admiration. "Did she grow up with you or her mother?" she asked, steering the conversation back into safer waters.

"Laura was eleven when we divorced. She lived with her mother for the first two years, and then she came to live with me after her mother remarried and left the country to start her new life."

"That must have been hard on her," Jo presumed.

The look in Daniel's eyes and the way he grimaced confirmed that it had been. "It was," he responded. "She was becoming this young woman with so many different emotions coming out of her, and I didn't know how to help her. I had to take her to therapy, but that didn't really help." He sighed, his gaze turning back to the water.

Jo looked over at the man choosing to be vulnerable before her, and all she wanted was to wrap her arms around his shoulders and pull him into her embrace to offer him comfort.

"I'm sorry you had to go through that. I know what it's like dealing with a highly emotional teenager," she expressed, her eyes glazing over with sadness as she remembered her own past behavior.

She looked at the hand on top of her hand resting on the armrest of the chair, reveling in the warm tingle running up her forearm. She looked up at the owner of the hand, staring at her with gratitude.

"I like this," he said simply.

Jo gave him a quizzical look.

"I like having you here, talking to you. I don't know what it is, but I just feel this freedom around you, like I could tell you my deepest, darkest secret, and it would be safe with you."

She widened her eyes at the revelation, and her heart started to beat erratically against her chest as she felt the warmth from his hand against hers traveling further up her arm toward her neck and cheeks.

"I know you said we can only be friends right now, and I respect that, but I just needed you to know how you make me feel."

Jo's lips parted to release a soft gasp. "You—"

"Dad?"

Jo quickly moved her hand from under Daniel's hand, and her face heated with embarrassment. She slightly turned in her chair to see a young woman standing by the back door, who was already staring at her with interest, her steel-gray eyes so reflective of the man sitting beside Jo.

"Hi, sweet pea. I didn't know you were coming here today," Daniel spoke brightly as he rose from his seat to go to her.

The young woman's gaze switched from Jo toward her father and a broad, warm smile graced her lips.

"Hi, Daddy," she said breathily the second Daniel stood in front of her and wrapped her in his arms.

Jo noticed that her head was resting just under his chin. She had to be about five feet nine inches or five feet ten inches tall.

"I came to invite you to lunch with me and Jeff. I wasn't expecting that you would have a guest," the young woman said, looking from her father to Jo, who was now standing and gripping the back of the chair as she stood in awkwardness.

"Let me introduce you," Daniel replied, turning in Jo's direction.

Jo felt her heartbeat pick up speed and her hand gripping the chair began to slacken as moisture sprung in her palm.

"Laura, this is Josephine Hamilton Boyer."

"Well, I'm glad to know my assumptions weren't off," the woman replied with a glint in her eyes as she smirked up at her father before flashing Jo a broad smile. "Hi, I'm Laura. It's nice to finally meet you and put a face to the name."

"Hi, it's nice to meet you as well," Jo replied, taking the hand Laura offered, giving her an uncertain smile before looking back at Daniel. "You said finally meet?"

"Um, yeah, Dad's spoken about you a lot this past month. I feel like I already know you."

Jo stared wide-eyed at the young woman before fixing

Daniel with a quizzical look. She noted how he cast his gaze to the ground as he scratched the back of his neck.

"Good things, I hope?" Jo asked, trying to ease the awkwardness.

"Oh, yes," Laura confirmed. "He said, you're kind, you're a great chef, and you're thoughtful. I think it's because he li—"

"All right, Laura. I'm sure Jo gets the picture," Daniel interrupted, a reddish undertone forming on his face and neck.

From the glint in Laura's eyes and from the way she turned to smirk at her father, Jo could tell that she wasn't quite ready to quit yet.

"You said you and Jeff wanted to take me to lunch. Is he here?" Daniel pointedly stared at his daughter as if willing her to move the conversation in the direction he wanted.

"Yep, he's in the living room taking a business call," Laura answered. "Seeing as you have a special guest, maybe a rain check... or you and Josephine are welcome to join us." Laura looked from Daniel to Jo with a hopeful expression.

"That is a kind offer, but I think I have already overstayed my welcome," Jo gracefully declined. "I need to get back home, so you don't have to disrupt your plans for me. Daniel can still go to lunch with you."

"Okay, no problem. I hope you'll be able to join us at another time, maybe."

"I would like that." Jo smiled broadly at the young woman who was already smiling at her with such sincerity. "It was nice meeting you, Laura."

"It was nice meeting you, too, Jo," Laura replied.

"I'll walk you to your car," she heard Daniel offer.

"Thanks," Jo replied before following him down the steps and heading toward the front.

"Bye, Jo." Laura waved at her.

"Bye, Laura." Jo waved back at the young woman. "She's lovely." Jo grinned up at Daniel as they stood at her car. She was pleasantly surprised at how easy it had been to fall into conversation with Laura. It had been so easy to talk to her, and Jo couldn't help the feeling that the young woman was trying to hint at the interest her father had in her.

Daniel beamed down at Jo. "She is," he agreed. "But she's also very direct. I'm sorry about that." He gave her a sheepish look.

"I liked that about her," Jo confessed with a shy smile.

Daniel returned her smile. The two stood for some time staring at each other, neither making a move.

"Well, I'll see you at work tomorrow, boss," Jo finally spoke.

"See you tomorrow, deputy," he said, moving to open her door so that she could get settled.

"Bye."

"Bye."

With that, Daniel closed the door, and Jo drove off, looking in her rearview mirror at the man who stood in the same position watching the car. A broad smirk broke out across her lips, and the flutters of butterflies settled in her chest. She wondered how she would be able to maintain just being friends with the man if this was her reaction every time she was around him.

Chapter Twenty-Three

"Drea, have you seen Mom? I haven't seen her anywhere downstairs. I checked the porch, and she's not there either." Jo grabbed a mug from the cupboard and poured herself a cup of coffee before going to sit across from Andrea at the island.

"No, I haven't. Did you check if she's upstairs in her room?" Andrea asked, taking a sip from the cup she held in her hands.

"I did. That's the first place I looked, but she's not up there."

"Who're you looking for?"

The sisters looked to the entrance to see Cora standing there with an expectant look.

"Mom isn't in the house or outside," Jo informed her.

"Oh, I saw her on my way from the inn earlier. She said she was going for a walk and would probably stop by the garden for a bit," Cora informed them. "Also, Marg wants you to look at a few ideas she has for the guest rooms," she spoke, looking at Andrea.

"Great. I was heading over after I had my coffee." Andrea

drank the last of her coffee before rising from her seat and heading to the sink to wash the cup.

"So, why are you looking for Mom?" Cora asked Jo.

"No reason. I was a little concerned when I couldn't find her.

Cora gave her a sympathetic smile. "I worry too. "It's so scary to think about a future without her in it."

Jo shuddered at the thought. She released a sigh. "I'm grateful for the time we're getting to spend with her now, but to think that at any minute this sickness can take over her body and turn her into a complete vegetable is completely heart-wrenching."

"It is terrifying," Cora agreed, gaze cast down to her clasped hands on the island's surface. "But there isn't much we can do about it. We just have to make each day count as we're making new memories with her and the family."

Jo released another lengthy sigh. "I just don't understand why she can't see that being a part of a trial would be a good thing— something that could prolong the quality of her life." She got up and went to the sink to wash out her cup. She turned to see Cora still staring at her clasped hands.

"It is her choice, Jo," she said, finally looking up at her. "We might not agree with it, but if this is what will make her happy, then... we just have to back off. I kind of understand why she doesn't want to do it, though. If I was in her position, maybe... just maybe, I would want a good year to spend surrounded by the love of my girls and my family, rather than being a part of an experimental trial that very well might not work."

Jo folded her hands over her chest as she leaned against the sink, mulling over her sister's words. "It's just hard to know that all of this will be coming to an end soon." She exhaled. "Seeing Mom so fragile and vulnerable, I don't know... it just scares me a lot, and then I start thinking about Charles and Nick and Dad, and I just..." She rested her chin on her chest as she stared at her feet, too overwhelmed with emotions to continue.

Cora walked over to her sister and enveloped her in her arms. "It's okay, Jo—"

"But it's not," Jo cried in anguish. "I'm about to lose another person I love, and I can't... I'm scared, Cora."

Cora placed her hands on either side of her sister's face and raised her head to look at her. "Listen to me, Jo, I know this is a lot to handle in such a short period of time, but I also know that you're strong. You can handle this, and you don't have to do it alone because we will be here for you— Andrea and I and the rest of the family."

Jo shook her head in understanding, willing a smile on her tear-stained face. "Okay," she finally said. "I'll support Mom's choice. Thanks for the talk. I needed that."

Cora gave her an understanding smile before pulling her into another hug. "Any time, Sis."

"I'm gonna go look for Mom," she announced to Cora as they separated.

"All right. I'm gonna grab something to eat and take a shower. Jamie is taking me into town later."

Jo grinned as she nodded, then exited the kitchen and made her way to the back door. She took her time strolling down the path that led to the garden admiring the lush green meadow-like grounds and the forest of trees in the distance that created an imaginary border around most of the property. It was beautiful and serene, and when she made it to the garden's gates, she could see why this was one of her mother's favorite places to be. The entrance itself was inviting with brightly colored flowers of the vines that intricately wound themselves around the arbor above the wooden gates and glimpses of an enticing view through the spaces in their frame. She walked up the cobbled stone path and pushed the gates to enter. As she walked through the garden, she couldn't help but stop to plant her nose against the blooms, appreciating the light fragrant scent emanating from them.

Jo could hear voices further up the path. She looked up to see what looked to be her mother and Jamie standing under the trellis draped in ivy vines that formed a gateway to another part of the garden.

"Hi, sweetie," Becky greeted Jo the minute she spotted her walking toward her.

"Hi, Mom, Jamie," Jo said.

"Hi, Jo," Jamie greeted her back with a warm smile.

Jo returned the smile before fixing her gaze on her mother. "I thought I'd come and keep you company. I didn't know that you already had that."

"Oh, I just happened to see Jamie on my way here, and I asked him to come to look at the area where I want the new benches to go. And, of course, trouble him with a bit more work that can be done around here."

"It's no trouble, Becky," Jamie chimed in. "I had time on my hands anyway. I'm waiting to take Cora to town."

"Jo, come let me show you what Jamie's going to do for me," Becky invited her daughter.

Jo took the hand her mother held out to her and followed her toward a section of the garden that was bare.

"I want to put a waterfall or fountain here, but I want the design to be stacked stones, and I want it to end in a pond where we could have some fish."

Jo shook her head in understanding, already visioning exactly what her mother wanted. "That sounds like a lovely use for the space," she shared. "Seems like by the time you're done executing your vision, none of us will ever want to leave this garden."

Becky chuckled at her daughter's words. "What a brilliant way to become one with nature. I guess we'll have to move our bedrooms down here then," she joked.

"I guess so," Jo agreed with a laugh. She looked over to see Jamie's shoulders shake slightly as he joined in their laughter.

After another thirty minutes of Becky walking around the space and explaining her requests, Jamie left to go pick up Cora, leaving the two women alone.

"So... what's on your mind?" Becky asked her daughter after the two sat on the concrete benches surrounded by exotic rose bushes.

"Nothing's on my mind. I just wanted to spend some time with you," Jo told her mother. "How is your hand feeling?"

"It's a little sore, it scratches a bit under the cast, but it's not bad. I can move my hand," Becky replied, raising her hand in the cast as evidence.

"Just be careful, Mom. Don't put too much pressure on it. It's still a relatively fresh fracture," Jo cautioned.

"Sweetie," Becky spoke, lifting her free hand to rest on her daughter's cheek as she looked into her eyes. "I'm fine. I promise. I don't want you to spend all of your time worrying about me. It's a fracture, something that could have happened to any one of you if you were the ones that had taken that fall."

"You're right," Jo accepted her mother's statement with a soft sigh. "I know what you're saying is true. I guess it's just that... it's been hard to see you as anything other than a strong person. I mean, I don't remember you ever being sick, and now that we're finally reunited, you're dealing with this illness, and now this happened, and it has me scared," she confessed.

Becky looked at her daughter with understanding. "I know it's hard to accept this, and I'm not saying that I'm okay with what is happening to me, but I don't want you or us to spend the time I have left worrying about what is going to happen and not make any happy memories. This illness is completely out of our control. I want to spend the remainder of my time enjoying my girls and the rest of the family. I finally have you girls back with me, and all I want is for us to make new, pure memories that I hope you will be able to look back on and be happy when I am no longer here."

Jo placed her palm over the hand on her cheek and gave her mother a grateful smile. "I love you, Mom."

"I love you, too, sweetie."

* * *

"What is happening in here?" Jo asked the moment she and Becky stepped up on the porch where Aunt Stacy, Tessa, Andrea, and Jules sat conversing and laughing. She could smell an aroma coming from inside the house that tickled her nose and caused her mouth to water.

"Hey, cuz." Tessa rose to give Jo a hug before turning to Becky. "How is your hand feeling, Aunt Becky?"

"It's not bad, Tessa. It feels like it's healing nicely," Becky informed her niece.

"Great, great. If you feel any discomfort, don't hesitate to call me, okay?"

"I will, sweetie. Thanks."

"Again, what's happening here? Don't get me wrong. I'm happy to see you all, but what is the occasion?" she asked after bending down to hug Aunt Stacy.

"We're reviving our family weekend tradition of good food and a hand of poker," Uncle Luke answered her question as he stepped through the back door.

"Hi, Uncle Luke," Jo and Becky said at the same time.

"Hi, baby girl," he greeted Jo, giving her a tight hug before lightly hugging Becky next.

"I didn't know you were coming here today, let alone were planning a family get-together."

"I thought it was time, Becks," Uncle Luke replied. "I called Cora earlier, and she and Andrea thought it was a great idea, but you and Jo were out by the garden. We thought it was best not to disturb your bonding time," he further explained.

"Okay," Becky accepted.

"You said this was a tradition?" Jo weighed in.

"Yeah, it was. What you girls aren't aware of is that when Sam was alive, we had these weekend get-togethers regularly until it became a tradition. Most of the family usually showed up as long as they weren't busy or had other engagements. We play poker for dimes and quarters, a few other cards and board games, and Maria and I serve our famous beef stew and dumplings. We thought that, now that you girls are back and things have settled down that we should revive these get-togethers," he clarified.

"Wow, really?" Jo asked, surprised that the rest of the family had remained so close even after her, Andrea, and Cora's departure from the island. "That's wonderful."

"Stew's ready," Aunt Maria announced to everyone as she stepped outside, wearing an apron.

"Great, the picnic table is all set up," Andrew spoke up. "I guess it's time to take this party there."

Everyone nodded their agreement, walked down the stairs, and made their way to the side of the house where the tables were set up overlooking the harbor.

Chapter Twenty-Four

"Come on, Jo. Make your bet."

Jo looked down at the upturned cards on the table and then back to the two in her hand. She knew it was a high probability that her hand was not the highest, and if she made a wrong move, then she would lose, but that was the beauty of poker— it was a game of chance— you were either a risk taker or you weren't. If she folded, then she would lose the few quarters she had wagered, but good to play another round. She decided to do the opposite. "I'm all in," she said, pushing the remaining dimes and quarters into the center of the table.

Uncle Luke looked from the coins to her with a gleam in his eyes.

"Show your hands, please," Cora spoke from the head of the table, face stoic and eyes focused on the cards on the table as she embodied the role of a poker dealer perfectly.

"You first," Uncle Luke suggested, still staring at her and smirking.

"You go first, Uncle," she countered. The man shook his

head no.

"I have an idea. Why don't you both show your hands at the same time?" Jules asked, just as invested in the game as the others that surrounded the table.

"All right, on the count of three. One, two, three."

They both turned over their cards at the same time, and by Luke's look of shock, she knew she'd won before she looked down on his cards.

"You won," Uncle Luke confirmed.

Jo smiled broadly. Her straight flush was the highest hand.

"You're a natural at this," her uncle mused. "I've never in all of my days lost to anyone but your father. I guess the apple really doesn't fall far from the tree."

"Yeah, Jo. The only person I've ever seen beat Dad was Uncle Sam," Tessa, who sat beside her, agreed.

Jo looked over at her mom, who smiled encouragingly at her. "Well, this definitely proves that I am my father's daughter," Jo replied jokingly, which elicited chuckles from the others around the table.

"So, about the music festival next month. Who's going or not going?" Tessa asked the sisters as they sat in lawn chairs closer to the water. The older folk had opted to have a go at the small stake poker game.

"Are you kidding me? The Dixie Chicks are having a concert on Whidbey, and I'm not there? Unless my name isn't Andrea Bethany Hamilton, I will definitely be there," Andrea spoke with conviction.

The others laughed. It was a known fact that Andrea had been a die-hard fan of the girl band since they were kids.

"We can make it a girl's outing. I'm sure the other ladies would love to go," Jo suggested.

"Um... I... actually Jamie bought tickets for the both of us," Cora said, giving Jo an apologetic smile.

"And Donny invited us to go together," Andrea added.

"But we can still go as a group," Cora quickly responded, just not as an all-girls group."

"That's fine. I wouldn't want to intrude on the time you get to spend with the guys," Jo replied. "Tessa and I and anyone else who wants to go could probably go together."

"Nonsense," Andrea refuted. "I wouldn't feel good knowing that we went to the same concert in separate groups. Jo, we're still a family, and anyone who enters our lives will have to get used to us being together like this."

"That's right," Cora said. "Besides, I know someone who would probably appreciate being invited on this outing."

"Who?" she asked.

"Daniel."

Jo pulled back her head in surprise. "Um, Daniel and I are just friends. Nothing more," she spoke slowly, hoping she sounded as convincing to them as she wanted to sound to herself.

"I know. You said that before. I just thought that as a friend, he would appreciate the gesture."

Jo smiled thinly at her sister. Maybe it hadn't been a good idea to tell her the person she'd gone to visit a week ago was Daniel. She could see the wheels turning in her sister's head and the fact that she'd also witnessed the awkward tension between them just two days ago. She knew all too well that her sister was scheming.

"I'll ask him if he's not busy," she settled.

"Great," Cora brought her hands together in celebration. The look that passed between her and Andrea did not go unnoticed by Jo. *Yup, definitely scheming.*

Tessa, who seemed to have picked up on her sisters' mischief, chuckled.

"So, what about Jules? Do you think she'd want to tag along?" Jo asked Cora, steering the conversation away from her.

Cora looked over at her daughter, who was resting in a

lounge chair up on the porch, sunglasses over her eyes that made it impossible to determine if she was asleep under their dark lens, and then back at the woman with a look of uncertainty.

"I'm not sure if she'll be up to it, but I'll ask her."

The sisters gave her a sympathetic look.

"What about you, Tessa? Anyone that you could possibly consider taking to this shindig?" Andrea asked, once more changing the subject to safer topics.

When the day finally began to wind down, and the sky became tinted a dull, orange-pinkish hue, the extended family called it a day and prepared themselves to head to their respective homes.

"Today was lovely. I had a great time," Tessa spoke as she hugged each sister goodbye and stepped into her car. "Kerry and the others are going to be so jealous of the fun I had today," she cheesed.

The sisters laughed as they stepped back and waved goodbye to their cousin.

"I had a lot of fun today. I already missed them not being here," Jo expressed as they walked up the steps of the front porch.

"Yeah, I agree," Andrea added as Cora nodded in agreement.

"Hey, Jo. Can I talk to you?"

Jo looked at Cora in surprise. "Um, sure," she accepted.

"I'll go check on, Mom," Andrea offered, heading for the door.

Jo and Cora made their way toward the side of the porch with the swing and sat in it. The two rocked back and forth slowly in silence for some time.

"If I made you feel some sort of way or embarrassed you by my comment about Daniel, please know that that wasn't my intention. I'm sorry, Jo."

Jo was rendered speechless by her sister's apology. Cora took her silence as affirmation and continued to speak. "I just don't want you to close yourself off from finding love again. What you and Charles had was special, and no one will be able to replace that, but I also know what it feels like to love again after a loss, even though the circumstances are different, and I believe that there is room in your heart to love again. I—"

"Cora," Jo stopped her sister. "I...I." She sighed in frustration as the words refused to come out. "I wasn't embarrassed. You just caught me off guard by your suggestion, especially seeing as Daniel and I are just friends. I need us to just be friends," she returned, hoping her sister would understand.

"I saw the way you and Daniel stared at each other the other day, especially when you both thought the other wasn't looking," Cora said after they'd fallen into silence for a while. "I know that look. I have given that look and received it."

"Jamie?" Jo asked, already knowing the answer.

Cora smiled in confirmation. "That's why I think you shouldn't hide behind the hurt. You need to open yourself to the possibilities of being as happy as you deserve to be. From what I have seen, Daniel is a good man— a good man who is captivated by you. If your healing comes with love, then that is what you deserve."

The passion and sincerity of Cora's words touched Jo's heart and made her think. Maybe it was time to move on. More than a year had passed since her husband's death. There was no written rule that specified how long one should mourn. If she was honest with herself, though, she would admit that since moving back to Oak Harbor, she'd thought less about her deceased loved ones than when she had been back in Tacoma in her old house. Being around her sisters, her mother, and extended family had sped up the process of her feeling whole again. Daniel had been an unexpected but pleasant surprise that made her feel things she hadn't felt in a long time, and that scared her. Her mind was split down the middle. She felt like if she gave him a chance, the memory of Charles and Nicholas would start to fade, and they would no longer be as important to her as they had been when alive, but being with Daniel also felt so right. It felt as if their paths were meant to cross at the time they did.

"I'm scared, Cora," she confessed, the vulnerability causing her voice to quiver.

"I know." Cora reached over and hugged her sister to her side. "I'm not saying it's going to be easy, but take a chance. If it doesn't work out, Drea and I will always have your back."

Jo grinned against her sister's shoulder as she looked out at the water and the tiny dots that were boats in the distance. She could feel her anxiety slowly melt away. "Thanks, Cora," she murmured gratefully.

"Anytime, sweetie." Cora brought her hand up to cup her sister's jaw as they remained in the same position for some time, looking out at the bay.

The following morning as Jo walked to the restaurant to help Daniel prepare for the afternoon crowd, she couldn't help the butterflies that cascaded over each other in her stomach in a rapid motion the closer she got to her destination. More than once, she'd had to run her palms down the sides of her pants to get rid of the moisture there.

"Hi," Daniel greeted her with a bright smile the minute she stepped into the kitchen.

"Hi," she replied, her voice breathless as the butterflies clogged her throat.

"Are you all right?" Daniel stared at her with concern in his eyes which only caused her heart to beat out a wild tattoo as she tried to formulate her thoughts. "Yeah... um... I'm great, actually." She smiled an awkward smile.

Daniel smiled back at her, but the concern was still present in his eyes.

Jo quickly ducked her head and took her place beside him. "What do you need me to do?" she asked, not looking at him.

"Jo," she heard him call her name, his voice soft and worried. "If you're not feeling up to the work today, you don't have to. I know I am always joking that letting you go is not an option, but I need you to be okay. That is more important to me than an—"

"I'm fine. I promise," Jo jumped in to assure him. "I'm just a bit... nervous?" Jo looked up into the steel-gray eyes that were already steering back at her, holding her captive in their mesmerizing glow.

"Why are you nervous?" he asked, his voice lowered an octave, the cadence causing her heart to thunder behind her ribcage. She felt the single line of sweat that collected at her nape run down her spine.

"Um... there is a Dixie Chicks concert on the island two weeks from now. I was wondering... I was wondering if you would like to go with me?" Jo switched her weight from one foot to the next. She inconspicuously wiped her hand against her pants as she waited for him to speak but then quickly added, "The girls are going too."

Daniel palmed the back of his neck. "You're asking me on a date?"

"Not a date... per se... I just thought that maybe you would want to join us," she rebutted. When Daniel didn't answer immediately, it made her regret asking.

"Sure, I'd love to," he remarked with a wide grin. Jo released the breath she hadn't realized she'd been holding in. "On one condition, go to dinner with me on a date."

Jo felt her heart rate skyrocket once more, and an angry sweat broke out over her brows. "Daniel," she started with uncertainty.

"Jo, just say yes," he interjected, looking at her seriously.

Chapter Twenty-Five

"So, what are you wearing for your date?" Jo looked away from her closet to stare at Andrea, who was lying across her bed, looking up at her.

"Seriously, Drea? I thought you actually came up here to help me choose," she deadpanned.

"I am here to help you. I just thought you would have had some choices prepared for me to help you pick." Andrea gave her a pointed look.

"Ugh, this is hopeless," Jo exclaimed, throwing her hands in the air. "Maybe this wasn't such a good idea."

"What wasn't a good idea?" Cora looked from an exasperated Jo to Andrea.

"Jo's having a dress crisis," Andrea replied, sitting up in the bed.

"I should have just said no, I can't go. It's too soon to be going on a date. Maybe I should just call him and cancel," Jo rattled as her nerves got the best of her.

"Jo, stop. It's too late to cancel now," Cora informed her.

"Besides, there is no way we would allow you to cancel," Andrea added.

Jo couldn't help the childishness that rose in her and found herself sticking her tongue out at her sister. Andrea scrunched her eyebrows together, making silly faces in the mirror at her. The two had burst into laughter, lightening the mood once more.

"Jo, you'll be fine." Cora held her head between her palms and looked into her eyes. "You deserve this. Remember that." Jo smiled gratefully at her big sister. "Now, let's find you a dress to wear."

Half an hour later, the doorbell rang.

"This was a bad idea."

"Jo, stop," Cora reprimanded her sister, moving her toward the floor-length closet mirror. "Now, look how beautiful you are. When you make it downstairs, you are going to smile at that man, take his compliment, go out and enjoy your evening."

Jo glanced at her appearance as her sister had commanded. She did look beautiful. Her brown hair was swept up in a high, bouncy ponytail with a strong side part at the front and swept to the side. Even though she wore minimal makeup, the light blush brought attention to her high cheekbones and light brown eyes, and the rouge lipstick she wore made her lips look full. The dress Cora chose for her was a burgundy, knee-length wrap dress with high slits in the long sleeves paired with three-inch gold sandals.

"Go charm that man," Cora insisted against her ear as Andrea cheered. Jo walked down the stairs and to the front door with her sisters in tow behind her.

"Wow. You look... beautiful," Daniel complimented Jo the minute he saw her.

"Thank you," Jo replied, blushing, adding even more tint to her cheeks. "You look handsome."

Daniel smiled warmly down at her, which caused the butterflies in her chest to act up. "Good evening, ladies." He looked behind her to greet her sisters, who were all smiles.

"Hi, Daniel. Please make sure she has a good time," Andrea instructed.

"I will," he replied, his gaze back on her as he smiled warmly at her.

"Have her back by midnight." Jo turned to give Cora an incredulous look. "Just kidding," she smiled wide.

"I promise to bring her home at a reasonable time," Daniel replied. "Shall we?" Jo took the hand he held out to her, and with that, they were on their way.

Jo felt as if she was riding on cloud nine. She felt her cheeks heat for the third time. They were still warm, even though the chilly wind from the open car window was caressing them. They drove in comfortable silence for the fifteen minutes it took them to get into town, where they would be going for dinner.

"Did I mention how lovely you look tonight," Daniel asked, his gray eyes shining with the sincerity of his words.

"You've said it a few times, but that doesn't mean I'm tired of hearing it." She smiled back at him warmly. They were only officially ten minutes into their date, and already she was delirious. Just then, their waiter showed up with their entrée, and for the next few minutes, they focused on the meal.

"I told Tracy I was going on a date."

"Oh, yeah? What was her reaction?" Daniel asked, looking up at her in interest.

"Well..." she paused for effect. "She was ecstatic. She said she's happy that I'm opening myself up to the possibility of love again," she spoke, lowering her head. Feeling a warm pressure on the top of hers, she looked up into the kind eyes of Daniel as his large hand covered hers.

"Laura's happy that I took the step and asked you out. She likes you very much," he revealed.

A sincere smile crossed her lips at the news. She liked his daughter, too, and to know that she approved warmed her heart.

"So, tell me your opinion on this beef." Daniel raised his fork with a sliver of the pink flesh of beef attached to it. Jo stretched over the table to meet his outstretched hand and take the meat into her mouth. After a few chews and her face made up in contemplation, she set her gaze on Daniel.

"It's okay, I guess. A little chewy, almost on the tough side. I'd rate it about a two or if I'm being generous, a three."

Daniel nodded in agreement. "You're spot-on." He beamed.

"Try this then," she invited, holding up her fork with the lamb chop she had ordered. Daniel took the piece of meat into his mouth and chewed.

"This is a bit chewy, overcooked, and too many spices."

"See? We make the perfect team." Daniel smiled at her tenderly.

"It seems we do." She smiled back at him. From there, their conversations went into what cooking schools they attended.

"L'Atelier des Sens?" Jo looked at Daniel, bug-eyed. "That's one of the most prestigious culinary schools," she fawned.

"I know, but it's overrated. It's not better than any other culinary school with exceptional instructors," he refuted.

"I still wish I'd had the privilege to go there."

"You're an exceptional sous-chef, Jo. I don't need a decorative piece of paper to see that," he complimented her.

"Seeing as the meal didn't live up to the hype, maybe we should forgo ordering dessert. I have a mean chocolate fudge cake and an excellent bottle of wine back home if you're interested," Jo invited.

"That sounds like a much better way to spend the rest of our evening," he agreed.

After paying the bill, the two left for her house.

"You two are back early. Did something happen?" Cora asked in surprise the minute they walked through the door.

"No, we just thought it would be better to finish our time together here eating the chocolate fudge cake I made," she explained.

"That's a great idea. Maybe Jamie and I should join you guys and help finish it inadequate time," Cora suggested. The two women looked back at Daniel and Jamie by the stairs having a conversation.

"Sounds like a good plan to me," Jo approved.

"Why don't you guys get settled out on the back porch? We'll take the cake and wine out to you," Cora instructed the men.

Thirty minutes later, they were laughing and making jokes as they sat out on the porch, the dimmed lantern lights casting a hazy glow over the space. "We're gonna leave you two now to finish your date. Jamie and I need to discuss something important," Cora stated to both of them. With that, she and Jamie went inside the house.

"So, I heard about Becky's illness... I'm sorry, Jo. I know how hard it is to watch a loved one deteriorate from an illness that is incurable," he empathized. The look in his eyes told her that he had his own experience. As if reading her mind, he answered. "My mom's kidneys failed her. She lived on dialysis for four years before she died."

Jo reached out and ran a comforting hand along his arm. "I'm sorry for your loss," she sympathized. After some time, they settled into a comfortable silence. Somehow Jo's hand slipped down Daniel's arm until their fingers intertwined, and it felt nice. It felt right.

"I had a wonderful time tonight, Daniel." Jo smiled softly at the man leaning against the door, staring down at her.

"Does that mean I get another date?"

"The verdict's still out on that," she returned with a slight grin.

"Well then, I'll just have to make sure I secure that 'yes' then, don't I?" He smirked.

"And how are you going to do that?"

Jo knew what was coming when he lowered his head while looking at her lips, and unlike last time the anticipation she felt was from waiting for his lips to meet hers. When his lips finally brushed across hers, she didn't resist but instead allowed him to draw her closer as she kissed him back. When they separated, her lips were tingling and warm from the pressure of his having been there, and goose bumps ran along her arms.

"I guess I got my answer then." Daniel beamed down at her, and she felt just about ready to become a puddle on the floor.

"Good night, Jo."

"Good night." She breathed silently.

Daniel turned and walked down the porch to get to his car. Jo watched him until the car pulled out of the driveway, then she closed the door and leaned against it. A broad smile broke out on her lips, and her chest felt warm. That night she had a peaceful, dreamless sleep.

* * *

Jo woke up feeling refreshed. She stretched languidly, a smile blossoming on her lips, as memories from the night before came seeping into her mind. She put the pad of her index and middle fingers against her mouth, remembering how firm his lips had been against hers. A flush came to her cheeks as the telltale fluttering started up in her stomach. Slowly, she swung her feet over the side of the bed and made her way toward the bathroom to freshen up for the day. She knew her family would be coming over as they'd promised last week that this would be the new routine for Sundays. She probably needed to be ready to go help her sisters prepare for their arrival.

Jo could hear voices coming from the kitchen, and the smell of freshly brewed coffee hit her nostrils, waking her up more than she was.

"Uncle Luke, Aunt Maria, you're here," she greeted, surprised the minute she entered the kitchen and saw them. "I didn't know you were coming here so early." She noted the trays of food already on display and had to look at the wall clock to confirm she hadn't slept half the day away. It was a little past eight in the morning.

"We figured you'd be wiped out from your date last night, so we decided to just get an early start on things," he explained, pulling her into a tight hug.

"She was wiped out all right. Literally half of her lipstick," Cora teased. Jo stared daggers into her sister, mortified by her comment. She couldn't believe she actually watched them.

"Don't tease your sister, sweetheart," Becky joined in. "Besides, he is a lovely young man," she praised Daniel, turning to give her daughter a warm smile. "Samuel liked him very much too. I know he would have approved of you two, as I have."

"Thanks, Mom." Jo wrapped her mother, who was smaller than her, into her arms.

"All right. I'm here now, everyone. The party can get started."

Everyone turned to look at Kerry, who had stacks of pastry boxes in her hands while she sported a wide smirk.

"I raided my shop, and I brought croissant rolls, Danish, and raspberry strudels... you know this isn't a get-together without a little bit of sweetness."

At this, everyone laughed heartily. Before long, the party had moved outside. Some were playing poker while others just sat and talked. A broad, appreciative smile came over Jo's face as she looked out across the vast expanse of her family and how everyone was having a wonderful time. It warmed her heart to the fullest. Coming home had been the best decision she'd made in a very long time.

Epilogue

"All right, everyone's got their tickets, right?" Andrea looked around the room at her family and friends with satisfaction as she received nods of confirmation.

"Great, we leave in the next fifteen minutes. Did anyone get an update from Ben? How far away he is right now?"

Jo looked over at Marg, looking back at Andrea wide-eyed. "No, I haven't. I thought he would have informed you?" Her last statement was more of a question.

"No, he didn't. Let me call him."

"Sorry, I'm late, guys. I had a client today that I almost had to bend over backward to accommodate, but I'm here now. What did I miss?"

"Almost the whole concert," Andrea muttered, looking at her cousin through the side of her eye.

Jo chuckled at how serious her sister got whenever it came to going to a concert put on by her favorite band. She could turn into a diva, literally.

"All right, Drea. Everything will be okay. Stop worrying," Jo encouraged her.

"I'm not worried. I just want us to stick to the schedule I set for us to make it there on time to get the best spots for viewing," Andrea reasoned.

"And we will. We aren't, of course," Jo countered, trying to calm her sister's nerves. She looked over at Marg, who seemed to want to crawl out of her skin and run away. She noticed Ben walking over to her and saying something to her. Finally, a smile broke out as she shook her head, and this caused Jo to smile. Maybe there could be something there.

She looked over at Cora and Jamie, already laughing in their own bubble. Donny had his hand on Andrea's shoulder, his fingers seemingly kneading out the tension.

Kerry and Tessa were laughing and joking with Becky and Jules, which brought another warm smile to her lips.

She felt a slight, warm pressure on her fingers and looked down to see that Daniel had entwined their fingers. He smiled tenderly down at her. Her fingers tingled with heat all the way up her arm and over her neck, flushing her cheeks slightly pink. Memories of their kiss from their last date were ever-present in her thoughts, and she just couldn't wait until he acted upon his feelings again.

Looking around at everyone once more, a soft grin graced her lips as she realized that this was the best place for her to be because this room was filled with love and affection and the evidence of restored relationships. In this room was the beginning of beautiful friendships and the hope of a second chance at love and happiness. If she had stayed back in Tacoma or gone anywhere else, she wouldn't be experiencing what she was right now.

"Are you okay?" Daniel asked as he beamed down at her.

Without hesitation, Jo raised to the tips of her toes and planted her lips against his. She heard the gasps of shock and excitement from the room, but her only focus was on how good it felt to be reunited with him.

When she finally separated from the kiss, she looked up at the man that was slowly stealing her heart with a tenderness she never thought she would be able to give again.

"I am."

Coming Next

You can pre order: Absolution

Other Books by Kimberly

The Archer Inn Series

Connect with Kimberly Thomas

Facebook
Newsletter
BookBub

To receive exclusive updates from Kimberly, please sign up to be on her Newsletter!

CLICK HERE TO SUBSCRIBE

www.ingramcontent.com/pod-product-compliance
Lightning Source LLC
LaVergne TN
LVHW021537100225
803390LV00041B/774
9798201149826